The
Heronmaster

Alex McGilvery

Cover Illustrations

Wil Oberdier

ISBN 978-0-9959926-9-6

Table of Contents

Murder in the Woods 1

Teaching OneEar 53

Sammy 57

Madison's Meteor 69

The Heronmaster 135

The Illustrator 185

Acknowledgements 187

Alex's Other Books 189

Murder in the Woods

Bob wandered down to the marsh for a bite to eat. He followed the trail, not paying much attention to anything but the surface sounds of the forest. Trees creaked in the breeze. Birds flitted about stashing food for the coming winter or stuffing themselves in readiness for flying south. Nothing that mattered. His antlers broke off the few branches that stretched over the path far enough to tangle with them, adding to the noise.

Bob was at the top of his game. Other animals told him he was an ugly, short tempered creature, but since he was a moose, that was a fair description. The ladies liked him fine; and it wouldn't be that long before he started bringing them in.

"Hey, Bob," A squirrel ran out on a branch in front of him. "Where you heading?"

"I'm just heading to the swamp to grab a bite."

"Something's off today." The squirrel ran back and forth on the branch.

"What?" Bob squinted at the squirrel. "It's safe enough. Listen, no one else is worried."

"Telling you, something's wrong."

"Get out of my face." Bob swung his antlers and snapped the branch just after the squirrel jumped away. She swore at him as he ambled off. Had to admire her repertoire of curses, even if they were directed at him.

He was the majestic moose; he gave the rack on his head a heft. A very fine majestic moose indeed. Could hardly wait for the ladies to be ready.

At the edge of the woods, Bob stopped, listened carefully and tested the wind. She might be a squirrel with a brain hardly bigger than the nuts she ate, but she was one of the forest's early warning systems. It didn't hurt to be a little extra careful; not that he'd ever tell her that.

The breeze didn't carry anything but the stench of swamp. Geese flew overhead honking. Safe enough. Bob walked out into the clearing and squelched through the mud to the marsh. He was knee deep in the water when a duck paddled past.

"Hey," the duck said, "How's it going?"

"Mmmmph," Bob said through the succulent plants in his mouth.

"Wish I could stay here all winter," the duck said. "I don't like the idea of flying through the war zone. I lost one of my best friends last year."

"Tough," Bob said, and left it to the duck to decide if he was being rude or sympathetic. The duck quacked and flew off. Bob guessed he had decided on rude. It just meant he could eat in peace before the sun came all the way up and made it too warm.

He gorged himself on the tender plants of the marsh. This was his favourite time of the year. He carried a full rack. He felt strong and sexy and soon the ladies would be coming and begging him for what only he could give them. It was also as safe as the forest ever got. Nobody wanted to mess with a bull moose.

Bob's head came up and he tested the wind. Maybe it was just thinking about the ladies but he was sure he'd got a whiff of a horny cow. Early in the season, sure, but not impossible. What better way to finish his breakfast than with some great sex?

Bob followed the scent deeper into the swamp. It got stronger. Thoughts of what he was going to do to this lovely lady flooded his head. She grunted from the thicket. She was as horny as him, and just around the bend. Oh boy, was he ready to do his part!

The rattle of some other moose's antlers came from the trees ahead. Immediately, he went from horny to enraged. No punk interloper was going to snatch this moment from him. He bellowed and ran forward. Water, plants and mud flew away from him. Bob was the most powerful inhabitant of the woods and no one, not even another bull moose, could go head to head with him.

Water and mud splashed as he charged into a clearing and looked around for his rival. A sharp pain stabbed his ribs but Bob pushed it aside. Nothing mattered but getting to that horny cow before anyone else. Another pain spiked through him and he stumbled for a moment. His feet refused to stay under him. They collapsed and dropped him into the water. The weight of his antlers held his head under. He needed to breathe, but didn't have the strength.

The last thing he felt was cold and sharp on his throat.

*****

Nick munched on a mouse that had been too slow to react to his approach. The world was a dangerous place. A dog-eat-dog kind of place, or more accurately, a wolf-eat-mouse kind of place. Nick grinned and looked around for any other slow creatures. He wasn't really hungry, but would take what he caught. This area was too quiet now. All the meal-sized creatures knew he was around.

Nick walked along the path taking in the smells of the forest. The underlying scent of the earth had a richer and deeper odour than the rotting remains of some owl or hawk's meal lying under the browning ferns to the right. Too far gone, at least when he wasn't desperately hungry. Water to the left, but there was an easier access ahead and always a chance of a slow or stupid creature becoming his next meal.

At the watering spot, he picked up the musky scent of a cow moose, but didn't let it concern him much. A single wolf was no threat to her, and the cow wouldn't bother him. She could wait in the brush until he'd finished. As Nick crouched to lap up water, the immense weight of a moose landed on his tail.

"What did you do with Bob?"

"Bob?" Nick tried to decide if his tail was broken. No herbivore would get a yip out of him.

"Bull moose, really cute rack, bit dense but very good at what needs to be done at mating time."

"What would we have to do with a bull moose? Our pack isn't that foolish."

"He's missing."

"What's that got to do with me?" Nick pulled forward a little; he might slip his tail out from under her hoof.

"You've got a nose and an attitude. Find him or find out what happened to him."

"Why would I do that?"

She leaned a bit on his tail and a whine leaked out between his teeth.

"Cause if you don't, I and all my lady friends will stomp you into the mud."

"You bitch," Nick tried to twist around far enough to get his teeth into the her. He wondered if his tail was going to come right off.

"I'm a moose," She leaned a little more, "The bitches are your kind. You find out what happened to Bob, or you're a mud puddle."

"How do I find you if I learn what's happened?"

"Like I said, you're the one with the nose." The cow lifted her hoof from Nick's tail. "You want me, ask for Irma." She walked off through the woods leaving Nick's tail aching. An experimental wag sent pain shooting up his back.

"Stupid cow," Nick held his tail carefully as he went back to the den to talk to the pack. He smelled several small animals and even saw a squirrel run in front of him; but he was afraid to hunt and bump his tail.

The sun was at its height. The Alpha would be lying by the den soaking up the heat, planning a hunt for the night, maybe even moose. Nick occupied himself with fantasies of dragging Irma to the ground and tasting her hot, rich blood flowing between his teeth.

The only wolf lying in the sun was Jen, a young bitch who flipped an ear at him when he came out of the bracken.

"Where's the Alpha?"

"Sleeping," she said, "like any sensible wolf."

"Hmmph," Nick said and tried to find a way to lie down that didn't send spikes of agony through his tail.

"What are you doing?" Jen asked.

"My tail hurts," Nick said, then yelped when he bumped against a tree.

"What happened?"

"Some cow moose named Irma stepped on it."

"A moose stepped on your tail?" Jen snorted and covered her muzzle with her paws trying to keep her laughter quiet, but her shaking body gave her away. She lost the battle and howled while rolling helplessly down the sandy bank. Nick tried to pounce on her, but his tail kept bumping into trees or the bank and he'd yelp. Every time he yelped she'd howl louder.

"What's all this ruckus?" The Alpha crawled out of the den.

Jen and Nick immediately crouched respectfully. Nick couldn't help a small whimper as his tail twinged.

"Nick's tail's hurt," Jen almost howled again.

"A moose stepped on it." He resented the need to explain something so humiliating to the Alpha.

"A moose stepped on your tail?" the Alpha said, "Were you sleeping with your tail on the path?" Something strange was happening to the lead wolf--suddenly howls of laughter erupted from him. Jen joined in, then the other wolves as they crawled out of the den and heard the story.

Nick buried his nose under his paws and tried not to whine like a puppy. Then he felt a cold nose nuzzling at him.

"Get up, Nick," the Alpha said. "You'd better tell us the whole story."

Nick looked up at him. The Alpha's jaw still dropped in amusement, but there was understanding in the old wolf's eyes which helped Nick stand. Just as he did sharp teeth latched onto his tail. They gave a hard pull and something snapped. He let out a long howl of agony and the rest of the pack joined him. Nick connected as he always did with the pack. His howl went from agony to laughter as he realized the pain was all but gone.

The pack stopped howling and looked at him expectantly.

"I went to get a drink at the creek where the sundown trail crosses it. I scented a cow moose, but I wasn't hungry so I didn't pay it much mind. Next thing the crazy cow had her big hoof planted on my tail and wouldn't let up. She figured I should know what killed her friend, a bull named Bob. I told her even we didn't mess with bulls around this time. She just crushed my tail harder and told me I'd better find out what happened to him or she'd find me and stomp me into mud."

The other wolves growled.

"Prey animals don't tell us what to do."

"We should go hunt her down."

"We're a pack, no grass eater can challenge us."

The Alpha stood up. Instantly the pack went silent.

"How many of you have hunted moose in the fall? Adult moose, not barely grown calves." The wolves put their noses down. "Yes, we would probably take her down but not easily. She'd kill at least one of us, perhaps more. What if she has friends who help her? Are you willing to attack a herd of moose?" They crouched to the ground and whined.

"So, what do we do?" Nick asked.

"I'm thinking you'd better go look for Bob," the Alpha said. Nick opened his mouth to argue, but the Alpha looked him in the eye. "For the good of the pack, Nick."

"For the good of the pack," Nick echoed.

"In the winter, Nick, the snow is deep and everything changes. For now, we keep the cows happy..." the Alpha's jaw dropped in humour again. "...and off our tails."

Nick ducked his head at the Alpha then headed toward the swamp.

"Where you going?" Jen asked as she fell into step with him.

"The swamp."

"What for? It's the wrong time of day for frogs."

"I'm thinking like a moose."

"Ha ha, right," Jen said, "So what does a moose think about?"

"Food," Nick said, "and their food is in the swamp right now."

Jen went quiet as they followed the trail to the swamp. The sweetish perfume of poplar gave way to the sharp scents of spruce and cedar. Moss and needles covered the damp ground. Nick detected rancid water; they were close. He sat and breathed in the other odours surrounding him. A rabbit holed up somewhere to his right. An owl left droppings over on the other side of the path, probably the rabbit's kin. The strong musk of moose remained from early in the morning, and squirrel.

"Wait here a minute." Nick moved up the path to where the squirrel scent was fresher.

"@&^%!$%^&*" A chattering squirrel sat in a branch well above Nick's reach and hurled abuse at him.

"Hey, squirrel," he said, but was interrupted by another stream of cursing. He sat under the tree and waited. The little red creature kept up the invective and tossed a pine cone at him.

"Look," Nick said, "I can't reach you. I just want to ask you a question. Answer it and I won't hunt you today."

"Liar," the squirrel said, "Liar, liar, liar, no one listens to squirrel until it's too late. Then blame the squirrel for not warning. I told him it wasn't right. He didn't listen. Why would you listen?"

"Who didn't listen?"

"Stupid moose, thinks he's bigger than everyone."

"Well, he pretty much is bigger than everyone."

"Still, didn't listen to squirrel, now he's gone. Horny cows bellow and stand on tails. We know, we watch, we watch. Everything that happens we squirrels see." The squirrel chittered laughter at him.

"What wasn't right?"

"Don't know. The morning was angry. The time was wrong. What do I know? Wolf not hunt?"

"I won't hunt you today," Nick said. He walked on toward the swamp. Behind him the squirrel chattered, then a squeak and silence. Jen came up to him.

"Some squirrel ran out on the path and stuck its tongue out at me."

"I promised her I wouldn't hunt squirrel for the day if she answered my questions."

"I didn't promise," Jen licked her lips.

Nick shrugged then put his nose to the muddy ground. The scent of moose was still there. He followed it to the water's edge. As he expected the scent stopped at the water. He wasn't sure what to do next.

"Ask the duck," Jen said.

"What?" Nick looked at her and she grinned.

"I've never eaten duck."

"What will you do if I have to talk to a moose?" Nick asked. Jen panted then licked her chops. Nick laughed at her. "At least wait until I've finished talking with him."

He walked up to the edge of the water and called out to the duck.

"Hey, duck!"

The duck glanced over at him and quacked, but didn't get any closer to them.

"Go back in the woods for a moment, Jen," Nick said. "I think your drooling is making him nervous."

Jen huffed, but went back into the forest.

Nick hopped on a small tuft of grass and balanced precariously while he looked for the next place to bring him closer to the duck without making him look like he was hunting it.

"I hate this time of year," the duck said when Nick got closer. "I'm going to have to fly through the war zone soon."

"War zone?" The tiny clump of grass wobbled beneath Nick's feet.

"It's terrible." The duck shook himself and turned upside down in the water. Nick waited for his head to reappear. "Terrible," the duck said through the weeds in his beak. "I lost a friend last year."

"That's tough," Nick said.

"That's what that moose said this morning. I couldn't decide if he was being sympathetic or rude."

"He's a moose."

"Yeah, and you're a wolf, even if a strange one."

"Which way did he go?"

"What do you care?"

"I'm going to hunt him down and eat him." Nick said and let his tongue hang out.

"Fine then, either way there will be one less nuisance in the world." The duck turned upside down in the water again and righted himself with a beak full of weeds. "He wandered off that way." The duck pointed before going head down again as Nick started to retrace his steps to shore.

Jen came running out of the woods at full speed. She launched herself out over the water at the duck still bobbing upside down in the water. It righted itself just before she landed and took off with a squawk.

Nick made it back to shore and shook the muddy water from his fur. Jen dragged herself out of the water. Mud plastered her fur to her body-- so thick even shaking hard as she was didn't dislodge it.

"You're going to have to find some clean water and wash it off," Nick tried not to laugh as he jumped back.

"I didn't think a duck could move that fast."

"He's lucky you can't fly."

"I almost got him."

"Right," Nick snorted and rubbed his nose with his paw. She really did reek.

Jen spat a couple of feathers from her mouth.

"There's some clean water this way," she said. "Then we'll find some more animals for you to talk to." She squelched off through the mud. Nick followed her. It was good a direction as any.

As they walked along the edge of the marsh, Jen stopped to shake every so often, but the mud clung to her fur like burrs, stinking worse as it got drier and thicker. Nick made out the spruce and cedar around them, but the combined smell of Jen and the swamp drowned out other subtler scents.

Ducks quacked, blue jays called out to each other warning that wolves were on the prowl. The sun slid into the forest leaving them in blue dusk. Brief stirrings told Nick the small creatures of the woods were poking their heads out into the evening. They froze as the scent of wolf emerged from the funk of swamp.

Jen finally found a clean pond with a bit of beach to get into the water. The moon had risen on the other side of the swamp and put white edges on the reeds and trees. As soon and Jen immersed herself the smell of the putrid mud receded and Nick picked out some of the other messages carried by the wind.

"Wait here," Nick said, "I'm going to take a wander and smell out what's what."

"I'm not getting out of this water until I smell like a wolf again."

"Stay in there long enough and you'll smell like a frog," Nick said, but she didn't reply. She was trying to shake under water.

Nick padded further through the marsh. A faint scent teased him; like death and it got stronger as he went. He might find Bob and everything would go back to the way it should be. It wasn't Bob. The smell came from the remains of a beaver swollen and ripe with being dead. It had been dead at least a few days, so it wasn't part of the mystery.

He went on a little further and picked up another scent under the death stench. He dropped his jaw and laughed to himself. This was the explanation for Bob's disappearance. Irma wasn't going to like it, but that was life as a cow. He should go on and see for himself, but at that moment he heard Jen give a brief call so he turned and bounded away. He'd be able to find them tomorrow.

"Damn, Jeb! That was a wolf. I almost had a shot at him too. You must have moved and scared him away."

"Wasn't me, Hank. I've been silent as a ghost. You must have bumped the boat with your rifle when you picked it up."

"Damn, I've never shot a wolf."

"You can't eat 'em."

"Don't care, I want to kill me a wolf."

"Well we'll come back and sit on that dead beaver. The wolf will come back to it."

"That thing? Ecchhh."

"That's why you can't eat 'em. All that stuff about them being great hunters. Sheep and dead animals is what they eat."

"There ain't any sheep around here."

"So we sit on that beaver or something, and we'll get you a wolf. For now, we'd better get back to camp and help Dan with the skinning."

"Alright, but tomorrow we're getting that wolf."

"Quiet, Jen." Nick cocked his head and listened hard.

"Can we go now?" Jen said. "I'm cold and I still smell like the swamp."

"Well, I guess that's why we don't hunt duck," Nick said. "I thought I heard something odd, but it's gone now."

The two wolves loped back to the den.

"You should have seen it," Nick told the pack as they lay around the den, "I thought she was going to just fly away like a bird."

"I almost had it," Jen said. "I had feathers in my mouth."

"Can't eat feathers," the Alpha said. He sat by the entrance to the den. His mate, Nick's mother lay by his side. Jen's mothers lay beside her mate at the other edge of the clearing.

"Time to hunt?" asked Nick.

"Time to hunt," the Alpha said, "but stay clear of the moose. We don't want any more tails being stood on."

The eight wolves vanished into the night. Nick made sure that Jen wasn't following him. He wanted some time away from the swamp smell. He headed upslope and scented the breeze. The moose would be in the valleys with open meadows and young poplars. That was good mouse hunting and even rabbit, but the thought of moose made his tail ache and the Alpha had said to stay away. There'd be mice where he headed and maybe more.

He threaded through the trees following a line that was more a suggestion than a path. As the trees thinned moonlight shone through yellowing leaves to leave confusing shadows on the ground. There might be a mouse standing in shadow beside a light area and Nick wouldn't see it. That was fine. He wasn't hunting by sight.

Nick took in the rich scents that were carried on the cool night breeze; the underlying odour of soil was a mix of death and life, trees had their own particular perfume, and the flowers too, over there--overripe berries and the black bear gorging on them. He adjusted his track to avoid the bear. Smaller predators hunted too; fox and bobcat, weasel and skunk. A tiny death squeak told him an owl snatched a mouse from the forest floor.

Nick sifted through the layers of the air and found a scent that make him drool. Rabbit. He stood and let the air flow past him and built up a picture of where his prey hid, no not hiding, eating the leaves from patches of wintergreen on the forest floor.

He crept forward until the rabbit moving in small hops was visible. Nick wrinkled his nose at the wintergreen's strong fragrance, but drooled in anticipation of the taste of rabbit. Though his heart raced, he forced himself to be still. One of the random hops brought it close enough to Nick for him to pounce. In an instant, he was on the rabbit and ready to tear out its throat.

"Wait!" the rabbit said. "I can tell you something."

"What kind of something?" Nick kept his paw firmly on the rabbit. The rapid beat of its heart and smell of its fear made him quiver.

"You're the wolf that's looking for the moose."

Nick just growled in response and let saliva drip onto his prey's fur.

"He was seen chasing after a cow moose that wasn't there."

"Even a bull moose isn't that dense."

"There was a scent, but no cow, a call, but no bull. My year's mate's brother's cousin's last year's mate's litter eldest saw it."

"And what do you expect for this information?"

"My children are abroad tonight. Don't hunt them."

"And you?"

"I am prey rightfully caught, just be quick."

Rabbits, while tasty, were on the small side. Nick thought about what the rabbit had told him as he crunched its bones.

How could there be the scent of a cow without a cow? It didn't make sense. There must be a simple explanation. Tomorrow he'd talk to the moose and then it would be her problem. He licked the last of the blood off his lips and headed back to the den.

He woke before the sun and loped toward the grassy meadow where he was most likely to find Irma. The early morning air hung cool and damp. Scent didn't travel far in the still air, but sounds travelled from great distances, like he could hear everything happening in the whole world.

"Jen," Nick stopped and sat on the path. "You might as well come out."

She stepped out of the brush and shook the damp off her fur.

"I though you might want company, in case they tried to step on you again."

Nick just nodded and headed on down the path.

"Don't try to eat the moose," he said over his shoulder.

The reached the meadow as the twilight of early morning was lifting. Nick didn't see any moose, but he didn't expect to. Those creatures were about as paranoid as one could get and still go out to eat. They were prey, though very large prey.

"I have a message for Irma," he called into the still air.

"I'm hungry," Jen said. "I didn't get much more than a mouse last night."

"Should be plenty of mice here, just don't go too far."

There must have been plenty of mice, because soon Jen was hopping and crouching and occasionally there would be a small squeak and some crunching.

"What do you want?" a young cow moose said as she came into the meadow. "Why is she eating all the mice?"

"She's hungry." Nick scratched at his ear. "Mice are easier to catch than moose."

The moose took a couple of steps back from Nick. Jen looked up and grinned at her with a mouse tail dangling from her jaws.

"Just tell Irma I want to talk to her." Nick said. "We'll wait here." He pounced on a mouse that ran between him and the young moose. The moose ran off into the woods. Her crashing through the brush lasted long after he'd caught his second and even third mouse.

"Good hunting," Jen said after they each had caught at least two paws of mice.

"Keep hunting but stay close," Nick said. "A big moose is coming this way." To his surprise it wasn't Irma that stepped out of the woods, but a bull. The spread of his antlers was wider than Nick was long. Used properly they were deadly weapons, and this bull walked like he knew exactly how to use them.

"Are you the wolf that's looking for Bob?"

"Me?" Nick said and tossed a mouse into the air before swallowing it. "Why would I be looking for Bob?"

"Because some fat cow stood on your tail and told you to."

Nick nodded and licked his lips.

"Yeah, that would be a good reason. What's your interest in Bob?"

"Let him stay lost."

"I do that, Irma and her friends trample me into mud."

"If he shows up," the bull said, "I'll trample you into mud." He tossed his antlers. "I should crush you right now and be done with it."

"You want Bob out of the way so you can grab his harem, right?" Nick said. "Don't you want to impress the cows with your masculine prowess?"

"There's younger bulls..."

"But Bob is too much for you is he?"

The bull snorted and lowered his antlers. Nick crouched ready to dodge the charge he was sure was coming. Then a streak of fur came out of the grass under the bull and Jen fastened her teeth on the bull's masculine prowess. A higher squeak than Nick imagined possible came from the bull as he twisted and danced trying to either crush the wolf or throw her off.

"Stand still, or she'll bite it right off. Then where will you be with the ladies?"

The bull stopped and stood absolutely still. Nick could see the whites of his eyes, but the fear was rapidly turning to rage.

"Drop him, Jen." Nick shook himself then crouched facing the bull. "I suggest you leave quickly and quietly," he said to the bull, "I have no interest in a fight to the death here." He bared his teeth and growled. "But say the word and we'll go." Jen growled off to the side. Blood dripped off the huge animal, and Nick drooled at the thought of eating moose. The bull walked off, a little stiffly. He stopped at the edge of the trees.

"This isn't over wolf!" he shouted, then vanished into the trees.

"It's never over until you're rotting or digesting," Nick said.

"What a disgusting thought," Irma said as she stepped out of the woods.

Jen looked up at Irma and grinned.

"Don't even think about it," Irma looked at Nick. "What have you learned? It isn't that I don't enjoy watching Ted being humiliated, but you need to stay focused."

"Ted," Nick stopped and glanced back where Ted had vanished, but without the crash of a bull moose walking through the woods. He raised his voice a bit. "Ted was quite interested in me not finding Bob. It seems he doesn't think he's bull enough to take on Bob." A sudden crashing echoed in the clearing as trees swayed and fell.

"I don't think it's smart of you to be pissing off Ted," Irma said.

"I think it will be a while before Ted is thinking about pissing," Jen let her tongue dangle. It gave her a charmingly insane look.

"Well, as long as you figure out what is going on with Bob before Ted kills you."

"Bob is chasing after a cow in full rut," Nick said. "I smelled her myself."

Irma peered down her nose at Nick. "I find that highly unlikely."

"You aren't just a bit jealous, are you?" Nick said. "Some other cow is getting him first?"

Irma glared at him.

"I would know, we all would. It's early, not just by days, but by a moon. It would be.... abnormal."

"I smelled it myself," Nick remembered what the rabbit had told him. "Unless there is a way for there to be cow scent and no cow."

"It is too early for that too, and even Bob wouldn't be such a fool." Irma turned and left.

"They scared all the mice away."

"I think you ate them all, Jen."

"I almost got to eat moose." Jen looked at him and laughed. "Got a taste anyway." She bounded away and Nick trotted after her.

They spent the rest of the day dozing in the sun at the den. Nick's mind kept running over Irma's reaction to the rabbit's claim that there was a cow but no cow. It looked like she knew what it meant. She probably knew about the bull thing too. Either way, it was no longer his problem. His life, and his tail, was safe from the cow moose, though probably not from Ted the bull.

When Nick woke, the sun had dipped behind the trees, and the sandy bank was cooling. His tail hardly hurt at all. It was wonderful not having the threat of Irma's big hooves hanging over him. Bob had just run off after some other cow, and Irma was jealous. The love life of moose was far too complicated. Fortunately, the only thing he needed to worry about now was catching more mice or another rabbit.

The wolves split up again to hunt, Nick headed uphill. He had no wish to tangle with either Ted or Irma, and the swamp didn't appeal to him. He would hunt for one of the rabbit's relatives.

Once again he followed the scents of the night and walked through the boundary between the spruce and poplars. The moon lay down confusing shadows, but his nose and his ears gave him a sharp picture of the forest. Tonight, the forest was quiet. Even the mice weren't moving much, and he didn't smell any fresh trace of rabbit.

Even so, Nick wandered most of the night. The moon went down and he heard the disconsolate hooting of an owl which fared no better than him. Finally, he returned hungry and grumpy and threw himself on the sandy bank. Not that he couldn't deal with being hungry, but it was fall, he shouldn't have to be hungry. He ought to have gone down to where the moose were, and hunted the mice in the meadow.

He closed his eyes and sent himself to sleep, better that than ruminating about his failure. The warmth of the sun on the bank awakened him. The other wolves were flopped down and enjoying the last of the season's warmth. It wouldn't be many moons before they huddled for warmth in the stuffy den and Jen would somehow grab the warmest spot.

"Did Jen go out again already?" Nick asked.

"mmph," The Alpha lifted his head and looked about. "Must have." He sat up and gave a long howl. Nick joined in along with the rest of the pack. They sang with their ears perked to catch Jen's reply from wherever she'd got to. The only response was the silence from all the creatures the wolves hunted.

"Go find her." The Alpha put his head down on the bank and closed his eyes, waiting for Nick to go out in search of his pack mate.

Nick sighed, shook off his doze, put his nose to the ground and followed Jen's trail. It meandered through the forest like a bumble bee's flight. She started by going uphill, but on a different angle to Nick. There was an old rotten stump which held her attention long enough for her to lie down. From there she went downhill toward the meadow where they had talked to Ted and Irma. Nick hoped that she hadn't tried to get another taste of moose. His jaw dropped in a grin. Who knew a moose could squeak like a mouse? Her path finally took her to the meadow where it wandered all over. She didn't have much luck. They probably ate too many mice when they were there earlier.

From the meadow, she wandered down toward the swamp. There were only a few places where it was easy to move from the forest to the swamp. The underbrush was thick even for a wolf. Jen's trail brought Nick out to where she had tried to catch the duck with her flying leap. Her path wandered about as if she were trying to find where

28

the duck nested. It probably slept safe in some tiny tuft of weeds in the middle of the water.

Her path followed the edge of the swamp toward the rank beaver. He hoped she wasn't eating that, her breath would stink for days. Then under the stink of the beaver he detected another scent, two really. One was a whiff of fresh meat, the other made his hackles rise even though it wasn't familiar.

He forced his way back into the brush and followed the trail from where he was out of sight. It was slower going here, as he needed to weave over and under and around trees and stumps and fallen branches. Both smells were getting stronger easer to follow. At the spot where the beaver had been, something had dragged it into the water. Where the beaver had been, was a large bone with bits of meat still on it. Moose meat, That other smell was strongest here too.

Jen's scent went right up to the bone as Nick would have expected it to, but then it changed to blood and fear. Her trail led into the trees just ahead of where he was. He crouched and forced himself to go on. He didn't need to go very far before he found her, or at least what was left of her; something had cut off her head and paws and stripped her of her skin.

Fear and grief and rage poured out of him in a long howl. A duck took off, then a sharp bang, almost like thunder, but not as deep. There was a last despairing quack, and a splash. He didn't stop to look, but took off running the other way. There was something very wrong and he figured the moose knew more than they were telling. It was time to let them know that wolves were dangerous too.

***

"Did you hear that?" Jeb peered around them in the boat as if whatever had howled would come flying out of the trees to attack them.

"Just a wolf," Hank said, "Sit down before you fall out of the boat. At least it scared up a duck. Something other than moose to eat."

"I thought you liked moose."

"I do, but it's got to hang a while before it's proper."

"That wolf sounded mad, Hank."

"It was a wolf, they're just dumb animals. They ain't got feelings."

"I never heard anything like that. It was so close."

"It'll probably be eating that bitch you shot by now." Hank paddled the boat toward the duck floating in the water. "I tell you, they're just dumb, vicious animals."

"You think Dan will be able to fix up my wolf skin right?"

"It won't be the first one he's done. I told you that bone would bring 'em in."

"I thought we'd see a whole pack of them."

"Naw, they're probably killed some moose already. That's why there ain't enough moose any more, the wolves eat 'em all."

"So why'd this one come?"

"Greedy, she's a young'un, and they have to eat last. She couldn't resist a little taste on the side." Hank sat and pushed at the oars. "Let's get back to camp with supper."

"I'm glad we're on an island. That wolf will never find us there." Jeb picked the duck out of the water.

"I told you. It's just a dumb animal. It's already forgotten that bitch. Wolves are just cold blooded killing machines."

***

Nick ran through the woods in a line which cut straight through Jen's meandering trail. He ignored all the scents and sounds of the forest. Clouds covered the sun; the forest dimmed and the air turned cold. He arrived at the meadow and put his nose to the ground. He had followed Jen's trail to her death, now he was looking for an older one to lead him to answers.

Ted's was easy, the bull moose had come straight to them, then run straight away after standing in the trees at the edge of the clearing to listen to them talk with Irma. There were branches and even trees broken where the moose had taken his rage out on the undergrowth. He'd headed off deeper into the woods afterwards, his tremendous antlers doing surprisingly little damage. The bull couldn't help him, and wasn't close enough to interfere, so the wolf went back to the meadow and put his nose to work again.

Irma's trail didn't track as easily as the bull's. No blood trail, and she visited the meadow several times. Nick tracked her around many loops before he found the freshest trail. The canny old cow clearly didn't trust Nick. He grinned-- time for her to learn just how right she was.

He followed the trail away from the meadow. She didn't stay on the same trail for long, but switched from one to another. Her direction stayed about the same though. She headed toward a series of clearings; the result of a fire from before Nick's time. The wolves traveled through them in winter, threading through black burn trunks and white snow drifts.

Now, in the early fall, they were filled with tall grass and young poplars. Irma and other cows had been eating the tops of the tender trees and the sap's fragrance lingered. He found a bedding place, but not one of Irma's. The cow moose's trail wove through the long narrow meadow. She stayed to the fringes, occasionally crossing from one side to the other.

Her scent grew fresher. Nick moved much faster than she had. The burn in his gut pushed him since he'd left what remained of Jen by the marsh. Irma probably bedded down for the warm part of the day. Like the wolves, moose preferred the dusk and twilight to move. The sun was dropping rapidly and she would be on the move again soon. He wanted to catch her before then.

Nick loped faster as the scent grew stronger until he came to a spot where her scent diffused over a large area. He was close to where she was resting. Since her nose was almost as good as his, he didn't have much time to find her.

The grass here was tall, high enough for the moose to lie down and be almost invisible. Trails through the meadow crossed and re-crossed. Nick circled and sifted the layers of musk. She had walked around before bedding down, but hadn't left yet. He wouldn't miss a trail that fresh.

He focused on his hunt so hard, he almost stepped on the mouse. It squeaked at him and he snapped it up and swallowed without thinking. The sounds carried through the chilled air. Irma's weight shifted as she lifted her head. She knew something was wrong. Her movement told him exactly where she lay. He bounded through the last screen of grass and landed in a crouch in front of her nose. The fire in his belly wanted to rip out her throat. His head wanted answers

"Don't get up," Nick said. "Time we had another little talk." He bared his teeth and growled at the cow moose. She would take a few seconds to get to her feet. Time in which he'd do serious damage. Irma looked at Nick with what he guessed was loathing.

"I should never have involved you."

"No." Nick snarled at her and the loathing shifted to something else. "You should have left me out of it and my pack mate would be alive. You knew all along what happened to Bob, and now you are going to tell me."

"No," Irma's breathing quickened, "I didn't know, really. I thought you wolves had done something to him. Safer for you to look for answers than me."

"Safer!" Nick moved so close to Irma's face that she looked at him out of one eye. "Tell me about the scent of cows without a cow, or a bull with no bull."

"We don't talk about it." Irma panted as if she'd been running. "It's bad luck to talk about them."

"It's going to be very bad luck to not tell me," Nick said, "You had information and didn't tell me. It's time."

"We call them the Lost Ones," Irma said, "I don't know where they come from, but they stink of danger. Every year they come to areas around here and they try to lure the bulls with the scent of cows that don't exist. We hear calls from bulls that aren't there. Bulls, cows, even calves go missing or die in front of us. I had a calf just fall over and die right in front of me one year. He was just a year old."

"Tell me more about these Lost Ones."

"They aren't like us." Irma shuddered as if the memory carried more fear than Nick's hot breath on her neck. "They move on two legs and carry branches around. They look weak, they're deaf and nose blind, but they can see like a hawk, and they don't need to touch you to kill you. It's something to do with those branches they carry. If they point one at you, you're dead. And they kill everything. Birds, squirrels, rabbits, moose, even wolves and bears."

"If they are so dangerous, why haven't I heard about them?"

"You're young, and you've spent most of your life in this forest. For some reason it's protected from the Lost Ones."

"Why not stay here all the time then?"

"There are too many of us for the forest to support. The trees are taking over the meadows and we need the meadows to eat. Out there there are broad tracks of ravaged land, but they have young trees to eat. We wander back and forth, sometimes the season catches us in the wrong place and we die."

"The season?"

"The death season, when the Lost Ones come and kill us and leave our bones in the woods. The scavengers grow fat. The wolf packs out there follow the Lost Ones and wait for death to strike so they can eat."

"You said that it wasn't the right season."

"It isn't, I'd know. It's when we are ready for the bulls. That isn't for a moon yet."

"So something is wrong?"

"More wrong, there is nothing right about the Lost Ones."

"What else can you tell me?"

"Well," Irma shuddered more, "they have these horrible claws at their waists. They use them to cut animals into pieces. I watched them cut up my dear little bull."

"If you haven't told me everything, I'll be back." Nick bared his teeth again, "I may come back anyway. Wherever you go, I'll find you." He bounded off into the grass and headed for the den. He needed to talk to the Alpha.

The sun had gone; Nick ran through the dark night. He reached the den before the other wolves left for the night hunt. The way that they turned and looked at him told him that they had waited for him. Ears and tails dropped as they saw that Nick was alone.

When Nick tried to tell them about Jen, what came out was a howl of pain, grief and anger. The others joined him in the howl. They didn't know the details yet, but the loss was shared in their song. The moon shone down on the pack and their howls echoed off its face and spun in new harmonies across the world.

Irma heard the howl and shuddered in the grass nest where she still laid. Ted thrashed at the trees in rage as the howl roiled through the secluded glen where he had gone to heal his wounds and salvage his dignity. Small creatures all through the forest froze in place and waited for the awful sound to cease.

***

"Listen to that," Jeb said, "I'm sure glad that we're out on this island."

"Don't be a fool," Hank said and tried to find some more meat on the carcass of the duck. "They're just fool animals. They ain't dangerous unless they catch you without a gun."

"Even then they're cowards," Dan said, "Wave a stick or a knife at them and they will skulk away with their tail between their legs." He threw a leg bone into the fire. "The weather's changing, boys. There's space for another moose before in the boat, so it's up early in the morning for us."

"At least we've got all the hard work of packing done. Remember that Jeb, last night you leave nothing but your tent and sleeping bag on shore." Hank gave up on the bird and opened another beer.

"What about our guns?" Jeb gnawed at a wing tip to disguise his hands shaking.

"Nothing to shoot here." Hank slapped him on the back. We keep one in case a bear comes by.

"Finish your beers and hit the sack." Dan stretched and spat into the fire then leaned his loaded gun against a tree outside the tent. Soon the camp was quiet except for the snapping of the fire and the howling of the wolves.

***

The moon sank into the trees before the howl ended. Nick told the pack about finding Jen's remains. He told them about his conversation with Irma about the Lost Ones.

"You will not hunt the Lost Ones," the Alpha said, "If we kill them, others will come with traps and poisons to hunt us. They kill without thought, but they don't allow others to hunt them.

"An Alpha led his pack in a land far warmthward of us here. The land was fat with animals that were slow and content. The Lost Ones had divided their land into small meadows with wire that kept their creatures docile but didn't slow the movement of wolves. They hunted the small cousins of the moose, but the prey took shelter in the midst of the Lost One's slow creatures. The wolves decided that if they couldn't hunt their rightful prey, they would hunt what presented itself.

"The big slow creatures almost lay down and died in from of them. The wolves grew sleek and content. Then one of them was caught by cruel jaws. None of them could free their pack mate. When they returned in the night the jaws were there, but their pack mate was gone. Death rained from the trees above them, and only a few escaped.

"The few that were left hid in the deepest woods and licked their wounds. One went out to find food for his pack and brought back some meat. The wolves died, one by one in agony, their back broken by the Lost One's revenge. Only one survived to return cold-ward with a dire warning. 'Stay far from the Lost Ones'"

Nick crouched before the Alpha and whined.

"Is there nothing to be done?" he asked, "It is wrong that they can kill without retribution."

"They cannot know that we are here," the Alpha said, "For the good of the pack."

"For the good of the pack," Nick said.

"For the good of the pack," the rest of the pack echoed.

Nick told them how Jen had followed him and how she had taken on the bull moose and made him squeak like a mouse. The pack laughed and others told their own stories of Jen and her life on the edge of madness. None of them hunted that night, but they shared and grieved their loss until the sun started to rise. They huddled together and drew comfort from the warmth of the pack.

Nick left the den in the morning and wandered aimlessly through the woods with nothing to do. He wasn't hungry. The lack of Jen's scent stabbed into him. He ended up at the swamp near where Jen died. The rancid scent of the swamp rolled over him and made him miss her even more. Then another scent caught his attention. The smell that was all around the spot where Jen lay. Without thinking he bounded into the woods. He felt a burning pain across his flank and heard a bang like a small clap of thunder.

Once in the cover of the forest he turned, looked, and snarled at the Lost Ones. They were standing on some kind of small island. One was waving a stick and yelling at the other two. The island rocked and Nick hoped it would tip and they would be swallowed up by the swamp.

It wasn't to be. They made the one waving the stick sit down, then used other sticks to move their island away. For some reason that Nick didn't fully understand, he followed them on the shore. He kept carefully in the shade, and peered at them through the trees. The Lost Ones, left the swamp and entered the lake. Nick followed to the edge of the water and watched them move to a small island a short run's distance from the shore.

He lay there through the day watching the island. The wound on his back annoyed him, but he'd got worse wrestling with Jen. The Lost Ones stayed there through the day. In the evening the small island carried them back toward the shore. The island stopped in the middle of the swamp and the Lost Ones held their sticks and looked toward the shore. Nick backed away from the shore and ran toward the moose's meadow. He wasn't allowed to hunt the Lost Ones, but he could warn the moose about where the Lost Ones were hunting. No matter how they'd angered him, he wouldn't let the Lost Ones take anything more from the forest.

He reached the first meadow where he and Jen had caught mice while waiting for Irma. Remembering that made his heart race. The smell of moose near by might have been part of the memory running through his mind. A shadow rushed him from the shadows of the forest and bowled him over.

Nick rolled and dodged as massive hooves thundered around him. He was seconds from being dead, but his nose identified Ted as his attacker. The bull was doing his best to turn Nick into a mud puddle in the meadow. Nick remembered how Jen dealt with the bull. He launched himself straight up into Ted's belly.

Feeling Nick's teeth in his belly drove the bull mad. He spun wildly and tried to dig Nick away with his antlers. The combination of spin and antler finally tossed Nick into the deep grass with the taste of moose on his tongue. Ted was hardly scratched, but Nick didn't care. Fire burned in his gut. Instead of running away like any sane wolf would when faced with an enraged bull moose, Nick scrambled to his feet and launched himself at the big bull.

The sweep of antlers barely missed Nick and he sunk his teeth into the bull's neck. Once again the bull threw him off without him doing any serious damage to the big animal. Ted came after him and Nick had to dodge the huge hooves and vicious antlers. The fire in Nick's belly changed, it flowed white hot and made him something different than he had ever experienced. He didn't care whether he lived or died, but this prey animal that dared attack him would breathe his last before the night finished.

There were no more direct attacks. Now, Nick jumped in and pulled back. Sometimes his teeth drew blood, and others he danced away without any damage done. Ted spun and stomped at the wolf. When he tried to catch Nick with his antlers, Nick drew blood from Ted's nose. In spite of Nick's killing fury, they were evenly matched. Ted was unable to catch the wolf, but Nick wasn't doing any real hurt to the moose.

Nick had no idea how long they fought before Ted slipped. The bull spun too hard to try to catch Nick and for a second he went to his knees. Nick was on the moose, not at the animal's throat, but to tear at the moose's hind leg. He wasn't able to completely hamstring the big animal, but for the first time he did significant damage. The moose had to favour his back leg and was just a little slower to move.

That was the beginning of the end. Nick scored another attack at the same leg and tore out the entire tendon. Now Ted had only three legs. The moose tried to escape, but Nick was there blocking every attempt to run. Ted fell again. Nick tore out the other hamstring, so the bull fell to his knees.

Nick crouched in front of Ted and bared his teeth.

Ted dipped his head to Nick. Even if Nick walked away now, the moose was doomed.

"I was raised on stories that it wasn't possible for a single wolf to bring down a bull in his prime," Ted spoke between gasps of pain. "The stories were wrong."

Nick nodded his head in his turn. The rage dissipated and left him empty. He had won an impossible battle, but he no longer cared. Jen was still gone.

"I came to warn you," Nick said, "the Lost Ones are hunting down by the swamp."

Ted just nodded and dropped his head to the ground as if the spread of antlers was too heavy for him to lift.

"Don't leave it unfinished," Ted said and lifted his head. Nick launched himself at the moose and tore out his throat so fast that the wolf didn't get any blood on him. Ted sighed and fell over on his side. Nick howled again. He sent his rage and grief and triumph into the night.

The other wolves came to the sound of his howl. They gathered around and joined in. When the howl ended, they feasted. The entire pack ate until they were ready to burst.

"I would never have believed it," the Alpha said, "What made you decide to kill a moose?"

"He started it," Nick said. The other wolves laughed

"Stupid moose," the Alpha said, "tasty, but stupid."

They lay about the partially eaten moose for the rest of the night and into the day.

"I would have thought Jen would be the one to go after a moose," one of the other wolves said.

"She did," Nick said, "She showed me the way." He got up and wandered off into the woods. Jen had gone after a moose indeed, and she had done it for his sake. He wasn't finished with this. He loped through the woods to the meadow where he had talked to Irma. She wasn't there, but he put his nose to the ground and started on her trail. It led him back toward the place where he had battled Ted to the death.

Halfway there the scent trail led off in a different direction. He followed it to where Irma stood knee deep in water and ate water weeds.

"Have you come to hunt me too?" Irma said.

"No," Nick said, "I came to warn you that the Lost Ones are hunting the swamp by the lake. I don't want them taking anyone else from our forest."

"So what do you plan to do about it, are you going to kill them too?"

"The Alpha has forbidden me that hunt."

"So then," Irma said, "I will avoid the swamp until the Lost Ones are gone." She went back to her eating. Nick headed back to the lake shore. He lay in the bush watching the island.

The small floating island with the Lost Ones floated back to the island. The clouds were building up and the wind splashed water over the Lost Ones in their island. Waves developed whitecaps as the temperature plummeted. They carried things to the island and he wondered if they were leaving, but night fell with the small island still there.

Nick lay there until late at night. The pack would be sleeping in the den, or still eating the moose. He walked down to the beach into the water and swam the distance to the island--a short run, but a long swim. He made it to the island, but didn't step onto the shore yet. The Alpha had said that the Lost Ones were not to know that the wolves were there. Of course, they did already since they killed and mutilated Jen, but the Alpha's words were not to be ignored.

Nick walked carefully around the island until he found rock that led from the water up onto the island. Irma had said that they were nose blind. He followed the rock up to where he saw their strange dens. Regular breathing came from inside the dens. The Lost Ones were sleeping. To one side of the dens the bones of the lost moose hung from three trees leaning together. He'd had his fill of moose for the night.

Nick padded carefully through the clearing smelling the entry to each den. In front of one was an odd-looking stick with a stink that put his hackles up. His flank ached briefly in sympathy. This was one of the Lost Ones killing sticks. Nick picked it up carefully, half expecting it to turn on him and strike him dead.

The stick was heavy and cold. Nick carried it to the water and swam out as far as he dared before he dropped it. He returned to the dens, but didn't find any more of the sticks. He walked around to where the little island was attached to the larger one and smelled more of the sticks along with moose meat.

Everything but the odd little dens was stuffed into the Lost Ones' small island. It was attached to a large tree by a heavy vine. His teeth weren't good at cutting, but he gnawed through the foul-tasting vine. The small island drifted and bobbed on the waves, but moved back onto the shore. Nick took the vine in his mouth again and swam away from the shore pulling the small island after him. As soon as he reached the waves, the wind snatched the small island from him and whisked it away.

Nick swam toward the mainland, cold and exhausted. He dragged himself onto the land and shook the water out of his fur. He ran toward the den and his pack without looking back.

***

Through the night the weather got worse. Rain fell from the cold, grey clouds. Just before morning it turned to snow. When the three men crawled shivering from their tents, the fire was out and the ashes soaked.

"Jeb, get a fire started," Dan said, "I need some coffee. Damn, it got cold quick." He kicked at the snow. "We won't be leaving today. We'll have to get some of the gear out of the boat."

Jeb stumbled down to the shore where the cold wind sucked the heat from him.

"Hey Hank," he yelled, you tied the boat on the south side, right?"

"What do you mean?" Hank shouted back, "Can't you even find a flipping boat?"

Jeb didn't respond because he was staring at the end of the rope that used to be tied to the boat. The other two came to find out what was taking so long and found him pointing to the frayed end of the rope.

"Damn it," Dan cuffed Jeb. "Why didn't you check the rope?"

"Hank tied the boat," Jeb glared at Dan. "But that rope was fine last night when we loaded the boat. The wolves found us and stole our boat."

"Don't be a fool," Dan said. Jeb cursed inarticulately and swung a fist at the older man. Dan casually blocked the punch and drove his fist into Jeb's gut then pushed him away. Jeb coughed and tripped into the icy water. He gasped and choked until Hank waded in to pull him to his feet and push him back toward camp.

"Take it easy on the kid," Hank said to Dan as he walked by. Dan shrugged. He looked closely at the end of the rope. It had the same chewed look as the ropes he used to tie up his dogs before he switched to chain. Dan followed the other two back to the camp.

Jeb's hands had already started shaking, but he was trying to lay wood for a fire. Only all the wood was wet.

"Look," Dan said, "You need to get to the dry wood in the middle of the stick." He took out his knife and chose a good-sized stick. He set his knife at the top of the stick and banged it on the rock. The stick split neatly down the middle. He did a few other sticks before one didn't cooperate. The knife hung up on a knot and stuck. He banged the stick on the rock a few times before the knife twisted loose. He dropped the knife and muttered a curse as the edge hit a rock.

"What are you staring at?" he said to Jeb.

"Y y y your h h h hand," Jeb pointed, "It's b b b bleeding."

A deep cut ran across the back of his hand. Oddly, there was no pain. Red blood flowed into a pool turning the snow red. Hank tried to tie up the hand, but it wouldn't stop bleeding. The island began spinning so Dan sat by the dead fire to wait for the ground to settle.

The snow started again and the temperature dropped further. All three of them shook uncontrollably. When Jeb lay down and curled up, Dan tried to tell him not to give up, but the words failed to get out past the chattering of his teeth. He wanted to get up and climb into the warm blankets in his tent, but his legs refused to work. The wind whipped snow in his face. He could hardly make out the shape of Hank sitting across the dead fire staring at him with blank eyes. He closed his eyes and put his head on his knees.

One by one the men stopped shivering.

Soon after they stopped breathing.

The snow kept falling. A soft blanket covered the island. Softening the shape of the moose's bones, hiding all trace of the Lost Ones.

Teaching OneEar

Patience is the secret. The young ones come and ask me to teach them. They want the rush, the blood, the thrill. They don't want to hear about patience. OneEar no more than the others.

He came to me all puppy eager.

"Teach me to kill, OldOne," he said. "I want to taste blood."

I cuffed him and turned away, but he wouldn't give up. Where ever I went, OneEar was there, begging me to teach him. I was tempted to change his name to NoEar,. But, if patience is the first lesson, persistence is the second. I took him with me on my next hunt.

"Walk quietly." I instructed him. We loped away through the heavy forest. OneEar panting behind me. When he turned his head as a squirrel chittered from a tree, he tripped. I turned to stare at him, trying not to laugh while he tried to look like some other pup had made all that noise. The squirrel did laugh and OneEar growled.

"Later," I said, "Unless you are better at climbing trees than walking quietly?" I didn't wait for a reply but walked on. OneEar followed; this time he watched his path.

We arrived at the edge of a pond. I lay down and waited. I didn't have to wait long.

"Now what?" OneEar said after drinking his fill, "Let's hunt!"

"We are hunting."

"Hunting what?"

"Frogs."

"Yech!" OneEar said, "Let's go hunt deer."

"Catch me a frog, and we will look for deer."

OneEar yelped with glee and pounced into the water. He sent up great splashes of water and mud as he lunged one way and another. Green frogs hopped and swam in all directions, but he didn't catch a single one. He stopped, still in the water, with green weeds draped across his face. Mud dripped from his fur.

I let my tongue hang out and laughed a little. OneEar peered at his reflection and laughed with me. He walked out of the water and shook mud and water and weeds all over me. Then he lay on the bank and watched me.

I waited for him to speak, but he stayed silent. The water stilled. As the mud settled one green head after another appeared. The young one quivered, but still, he waited. A breeze blew tiny footprints across the water. Birds called from the tree behind us. Flies appeared and settled on our backs. Still, he waited.

First one frog than another climbed out of the pond. They were on their own hunt, eating the flies that were biting at us. A huge fat green frog hopped up almost to OneEar's nose. With a snap the pup jumped on the bullfrog and snapped it up.

I barked with approval as he stood with the frog's legs flailing on either side of his mouth.

"How does it taste?" I asked.

"Green," OneEar said, "And cold."

"Still food," I said, "Eat him, you will need the strength for the deer."

OneEar shook his head, and with a snap and gulp the frog vanished. I laughed at his expression--as if the frog still swam around in his stomach.

"Deer,"

"Follow very quietly," I led the way along the shore of the pond to the meadow where the deer would come to eat at dusk. I made a point of checking the wind and picking a place that would be downwind, but protected our backs. Once again I lay down and waited. OneEar lay beside me once more quivering with excitement.

The sun was warm. the pup fought drowsiness, his nose dipping to his paws before he'd lift it up again. The flies found us and twitches replaced drowsiness as he stopped himself snapping at his tormentors. Squirrels rustled about in the bushes behind us while a small bird almost landed on his nose. The shadows grew longer, the flies thicker. Still we waited.

The light had become so dim that we could hardly see across the meadow when the deer appeared. One than another paced cautiously into the dusk. Yet deer are not frogs to walk up and place themselves into our mouths. I watched OneEar. I did not have long to wait. A fat doe followed the grass to our side of the field. The pup lunged out at her.

If she had been a frog he would have caught her. Instead she bounded away and he gave chase. He growled and snapped and tumbled through that field but didn't touch so much as a hair of one of those deer.

Finally, he came over panting and laughing.

"I think," he said, "I need to hunt more frogs."

I nipped him gently. "Let's go home."

"Can we catch frogs on the way?"

I laughed and howled my approval.

Sammy

I basked in the glow of my new car. She was a gem--a little red MGB--my last extravagance before settling down as a responsible adult.

We drove through one of those fragile fall days which held a painful clarity. The breeze blew cool and the sun shone warm. People moved on the sidewalks with a conscious briskness as if such a day could not possibly last and, if they stopped to enjoy it, it would turn to cold and rain. This day belonged to the adults of the city since the children were safely ensconced in school.

The MGB wove in and out of traffic passing secretaries and businessmen, storekeepers and shoppers. They formed a spectacle not as colourful as the dance of the falling leaves, but more purposeful.

I pulled into the park, quiet with the absence of children, but bright with the flame of maple leaves. An incongruous balloon pedlar vainly tried to sell his wares to the businesslike walkers and joggers. Apparently, I was the only person not caught up by urgent business.

On a crazy impulse, I parked the car and walked up to the man

"Only a dollar for a beautiful big balloon, only a dollar," he droned in a melancholy voice though none of this busy crowd had time for a balloon. I stepped in front of him and before I could change my mind I pulled out a tattered dollar bill.

"I'll take the red one." The balloon man paused in his droning long enough to take my money and hand me the balloon--the same bright red as my car. It bobbed eagerly at the end of its tether. Heat warmed my face at my foolishness, and I shortened the string as if that could salvage my dignity. A look at my new car revived my carefree mood. I chuckled as I tied the balloon to the antennae of my car.

"That's a fine-looking balloon you've got there." I turned and my jaw dropped. A small elderly man with thin grey hair and a wrinkled face wore the irrepressible look of a small child. He wore blue jeans and a gloriously loud Hawaiian shirt. Yet his smile caught my attention first. It stretched from ear to ear and showed a warmth most commonly reserved for good friends. His hand was stretched forward, so automatically, I shook it.

"My name is Sammy," Sammy said and shook my hand again.

"Oh, yeah." I closed my mouth with a snap. "Mine's Jim"

He shook my hand a third time then released my captive arm. Three times being enough even for Sammy

We stood long enough to exchange a few words, yet already people on the sidewalk circled around us as if they passed near extreme danger. We did make a strange pair, I with my red balloon, and Sammy with his joyous colour. The only people not going somewhere. The heat returned, but politeness kept me from leaping into my car and squealing the tires as I escaped.

"What's her name?"

"Who?" I looked around for the girl who had so precipitously entered the conversation.

"Your car," he said. "What do you call her? She's a beauty."

"Isn't she though, just bought her this morning." I stroked the hood. "I've been saving a long time to afford her. She's an 1980 MGB--spoke wheels, even a radio--"

"If I had a car like that I would call her Esmerelda." Sammy interrupted me shyly. "I had a cat named Esmerelda, but they wouldn't let me keep her."

We were surrounded by people hurrying to undoubtedly important appointments, but none offered any means of escape.

I ran my hand across the red fender of my new car. A laugh bubbled up from my gut, on a day like today, I didn't need to fit in. The heat in my face, the tension in my shoulders vanished. Today, I was not one of those people.

"Sammy," I said, "How'd you like to go for a spin?"

"Go for a ride? In Esmerelda?" He beamed even wider and nodded vigourously.

"Well then, hop in." I waited just long enough for Sammy to figure out his seatbelt, then we took off in my newly christened car.

I cruised through the traffic while Sammy waved at startled motorists. That mad, red balloon flapped in the breeze. Even in the middle of the day, traffic was stop and go downtown. A group of teens skipping school started a commentary on my balloon and Sammy's shirt while I bragged about my car. We took a block to out distance them. For everybody else, we were invisible, inhabiting the other side of a line few people wanted to cross. Before I bought the balloon, I'd lived on their side of the line. They didn't know what they were missing.

We got to the bottom of Main St. and turned onto Lakeshore. This was a different crowd. Roller-bladers and skateboarders rumbled along the sidewalk. They wove in between the mothers with luxury strollers and the joggers. Sammy got more responses to his waves. If he smiled any wider his head might fall right off. A snack-bar had a line snaking along the sidewalk in front of it.

"Hungry?" I asked.

"Am I ever. I could eat a horse!" Sammy rolled his eyes and laughed.

At the die-hard snack-bar I bought hamburgers and cokes. We walked along the boardwalk and talked of cars in general and Esmerelda in particular. The lake sparkled in sunshine and sailboats were out taking advantage of the perfect weather. Even with the cool wind off the lake it was comfortably warm.

Sammy froze and with a cry of glee he swooped on a coin lying on the pavement.

"It's one of those new dollar coins." He showed it to me proudly.

"Don't they call them loonies?"

Sammy winked at me and chuckled as at a secret joke.

"Good thing *I* found it." He laughed louder and held it up. The coin caught the sun and flashed bright like gold. But Sammy's smile shone brighter yet as he carefully placed his find in his pocket.

"I'll buy a balloon from the balloon man and let it go."

"Why?" *A strange reason for buying a balloon.*

"So I can watch it fly free and disappear." He sounded perfectly reasonable, but my gut warned me of dangerous ground. I retreated and changed the subject.

"How about an ice cream, Sammy?"

His grin was answer enough. Sammy and I walked to the beach to eat our ice cream and watch the sea gulls. They flew up to us and screeched, demanding that we feed them. Nothing would satisfy Sammy, but he had to find something to feed to the birds. Back we went and bought fries. He tossed them into the air as the birds wheeled and dove to catch them. When they fought over the fries Sammy chased them away, waving his arms and shouting.

"It's fun to feed them but they shouldn't be greedy you know." He said as he returned puffing from the chase.

All too soon, the fries vanished. Sammy chased the gulls down the beach one last time, shouting goodbye. He came back looking wistfully at the now distant flock.

"*They* don't let me feed the birds." A cloud covered the sun. The afternoon turned cold as we returned to the car. The balloon greeted us, pulling and bobbing in the wind.

"The balloon wants to be free. See! It's trying to escape."

"Well, you hold it for me then." I untied the balloon and handed it to Sammy who accepted it solemnly. The growing clouds convinced me to put the cover on the car. It'd looked a lot easier when the dealer had casually raised it. Of course, he didn't have to deal with a gusty wind.

After pinched fingers and words which made Sammy put his hands over his mouth, the roof was in place. Sammy and I climbed in and drove out into traffic.

Sammy cradled the balloon tenderly, running his finger gently across its red skin.

"It should be free," he said in a firm voice.

"What? Oh, the balloon. Why?" He stared intently at the balloon. For the first time since I had met him, Sammy wasn't smiling.

"It wants to be free, but we keep it tied down." He explained it to me like a teacher to a slightly slow pupil.

"Sammy, it's just a balloon." Deliberately I focused on the road, we were on opposite sides of that line. The burger curdled in my stomach.

"This balloon is meant to fly up in the sky so we can watch to see it disappear."

"But its only a balloon, Sammy."

"Doesn't matter, balloons or people it's the same," he said. "We should let it go."

I lapsed into silence, hoping it would be safer than words. Sammy looked at me then sighed as if I had failed a test.

"*They* don't understand either."

"They?" I asked. "Who are they?"

Sammy was covered with gloom, even his shirt no longer bright and joyful, but jarring and out of place.

"They keep me locked up. They don't like it when I escape. They always chase after me to lock me up again."

I signaled to turn toward the park.

"They don't understand." A whisper, lost in the sound of the wind. "Nobody understands."

"Why do they lock you up?" I asked, finally daring to at least send a thread across the line dividing us.

"Because I'm old," he said. "I don't want to be old. I don't want to work on puzzles with pieces missing and eat food that is carefully cut into tiny bits. I want to live life, but I'm not allowed. It disturbs the others. I go find things to do, but *they* get angry and drag me back. Why can't I live the way I want? I don't understand."

I didn't understand either. How had what started as a lark become so serious? Happy enough for Sammy to share my joy, but inadequate in the face of his pain. No words came, so we drove through the rush hour traffic. Pedestrians hurried with their heads down.

Sammy clutched the balloon and stared out the window at the people rushing by at a snail's pace.

The park had become a cold, dreary place dimmed by the shadows of office buildings. The balloon man had long since given up and gone. Even the flame of the maples was quenched by the gathering dusk.

As we got out of the car man with a harried look rushed up t and took hold of Sammy's arm. Sammy still held the red balloon. But where I had felt foolish carrying it, he carried it with dignity.

"Hello, Doctor," Sammy's voice was subdued, like a child caught skipping school. The doctor was dressed in a dark-blue suit, and wore an ID tag on his suit pocket.

"Where have you been, Sammy?" the doctor said. 'We've been looking all over." He glanced at me. "I'm sorry he bothered you. Sammy isn't dangerous, but he gets away from us now and then, and we have to chase after him."

He shot another glare at Sammy who hung his head in utter defeat.

"We warned you if you ran off again we would have to lock you in." The doctor rolled his eyes in exasperation and tried to pull me in with an expression which stated clearly we shared residence on the safe side of that invisible line. "He doesn't realize that we're trying to help him but he has these delusions."

"What exactly are these delusions?" I asked, a little more rudely than I had intended. The doctor glared at me, perhaps no longer sure we stood on the same side after all.

"He imagines that there are people chasing him to lock him up. He thinks everyone is out to get him, but he's not at all dangerous." He turned to his captive again. "Sammy get rid of that ridiculous thing."

Sammy handed me the balloon. I held on to it awkwardly and shook hands one more time with Sammy.

"Can't you just let him out once and while?"

"We take very good care of our residents," the doctor said, "We take them on suitable excursions, but we can't just let them wander the streets. It isn't safe."

"So you lock them up? You said yourself that Sammy isn't dangerous."

"We know what is best for our residents," the doctor said in a voice colder than the lake wind.

I took a breath to argue, but Sammy stopped me.

"It's all right, Jim." Sammy said quietly. "It was a good day" I shook his hand again. The doctor guided his captive away.

"Wait!" Sammy suddenly pulled free and ran back to me. "Here, take the loonie." I could find no adequate reply so I took the coin, then held out my hand. Sammy shook it one last time.

"Keep it for luck." He trotted obediently back to where his keeper impatiently tapped his foot. They headed toward a grey sedan.

I couldn't let the day with Esmerelda and the friend who named her end like this, not our day lived on the other side.

"Sammy," A young couple walking their dog turned to look at me

"Sammy!" People on the sidewalk stopped to see what all the commotion was.

"SAMMY!" All attention in the park was fastened on me. People began to edge away from the disturbance, but I was oblivious.

Yet, when he turned back to me, I didn't have words, he didn't need words. Nothing I could say would free him. The balloon caught the wind and tugged at my fingers.

"Sammy," I said, "look."

I let go of the string.

Sammy's eyes widened. He smiled at me and waved, then watched the balloon with childlike delight.

The balloon paused at first as if it weren't sure of its freedom. It bobbed and skipped across the park. Joggers and dog-walkers and men in suits stepped out of its way. The young couple's dog barked at it. It rose, hesitantly at first, then shot up into the air. Silence held the world as I followed its flight. It rose past the tops of the trees--the wind caught and swirled it in a mad dance.

The last rays of the setting sun caught the balloon, and it shone glorious red. Growing smaller and smaller until it was just a point of brilliant colour.

And at last, only the deepening blue of the twilight sky.

Madison's Meteor

Until the meteor fell, nothing notable had happened in the town of Madison since the year of its founding. The night it fell started cold and snowy. Nobody with any sense was out and about except for Frank Madison. He sat on the icy metal seat of his old Ford tractor driving toward the first of the driveways he would blow out. The owners of oversized piles of bricks hired him so they'd be able to drive their Mercedes and Jaguars off to their cushy jobs in the city. None of them gave Frank a second thought unless he was late with the tractor.

Frank had so many layers on that he had difficulty moving. It wasn't much of a problem since he was used to it. It did mean he had to look straight forward. That was why he saw the shadows first, then the intense light which cast them. They stretched in front of him as if one of those big rigs that used to come to the plant had plumped down in the middle of the road behind him. He couldn't turn to look back so he prayed that death would be quick. At least he wouldn't be so damned cold anymore.

The shadows shortened, but the crash didn't come. Instead, a ball of fire streaked over his head and smashed into the frozen field on his right. Frank felt a wave of warm wash over him, and without thinking about it, he turned the tractor into the field. The bumps and dips of the frozen furrows beneath the snow almost tossed him from his seat, but he persevered until he parked on the edge of a small crater that steamed with melted snow.

At the bottom of the crater a large rock glowed vivid orange. It dimmed to red as Frank watched, then even the red faded, leaving an ugly black rock that looked a little like the cinders on the rail line. Heaving himself from the tractor, Frank pulled out the chain that he used to rescue the cars that landed in the ditch outside his ramshackle farm.

The heat was incredible, but he got a loop of chain around the rock. It took most of the rest of the night, but Frank managed to hang the rock from the bucket in front of his tractor. He had peeled most of his layers off and was able to twist and look back as he reversed the old tractor out of the field onto the road.

The snow had stopped and the night was stunningly clear. Screw the Fat Cats, I'm going home.

He shivered as he parked the tractor in his shed, but still took the time to untangle the chain and leave the rock in a corner of the shed, covered with a tarp. It was cool enough now to touch. The warmth from the rock suffused him and his shivering stopped.

He felt reborn.

***

In the morning Frank rolled out of bed and made it to the door before he realized that the alarm hadn't gone off. A quick check of the alarm clock showed that he was actually early though he felt completely rested. He switched off the alarm and went to make his breakfast.

After breakfast were his morning chores. He whistled as he fed and watered the animals that shared his farm. He took great pleasure in caring well for his livestock. Since Frank had never married and had no children, the animals took the place of family for him. He knew that his father had hoped that he would carry on the Madison name, but Frank had never found a woman who would put up with him. With the plant closing, the town seemed likely to die, so it was reasonable that the name should go too.

Only after all the livestock had been cared for, did Frank return to the shed and the mysterious rock from the night before. He pulled back the tarp and looked at it. It was as black and ugly as ever, but something drew him to it. He put his hands on the rock and felt an echo of the warmth it had held.

"I don't know what I am going to do with you," he said as he looked at the rock from all angles. It was egg-shaped and about a meter from end to end. He tried to roll it over to look at the bottom side and couldn't budge it.

"Heavy beggar." A magnet stuck firmly to the rock, but when he checked, nails didn't. He covered the rock with the tarp.

Frank's truck was only slightly newer than the tractor, but it took him into town as it did every day. He parked it in front of the coffee shop and went inside. The regulars waved or nodded at him while Alice put a cup of coffee in front of him.

"Hey, Madison, you didn't plow my driveway last night." Bruce was the only local who hired Frank to clear his drive. He used to be the manager of the plant that had been closed by the bank. He still wasn't used to thinking of himself as just another person again.

"Nope."

"Why the hell not?"

"Not enough snow," Frank said. "Wasn't worth the trip." He took a sip of the bitter black treacle Alice thought was good coffee.

"I want it cleared out. Now."

"Nope."

"What?"

"I'm drinking my coffee." Frank took a long sip to demonstrate. "Maybe later, if I'm not busy."

Bruce looked like he was going to explode on the spot. He tried several times to put words together, but only spluttering noises came out.

"You're fired!" he finally said.

"OK." Frank took another sip. Alice's coffee was like that. It grew on you.

"So," Bruce said, "Who's going to clear my drive?" No one said anything, or even looked at him.

"The hardware store has a sale on shovels," Frank said. Bruce stared at him for a moment, then stomped out of the store. Alice came over to pour Frank some more coffee.

"I do believe that this is the best coffee you've ever made." Frank said. The warmth of the cup reminded him of the rock. It felt good in his hands. The other regulars held out their cups for refills.

"Shovels," one said, "brilliant."

Conversation turned back to its usual rut. The future of the plant. Every business in town had depended on the money spent by the workers at that plant. The new people didn't spend their money in town. They drove the half hour down the black top to drink coffee with fancy names and buy their clothes with labels that said Designed by.... Without the plant, everything else was going to die.

"Tell me again why they closed the plant," Bob asked.

"Wasn't making no money," Jim said.

"We had the best production record of any plant in the country."

"Too good," Herb said. "They couldn't sell what we were making."

"But they just put all that new machinery in." Daniel was one of the few young men left in town.

"Tax write off," Jim said.

"I wonder how much they will sell the plant for?" Frank said. All the eyes in the coffee shop stared at him. That wasn't part of the normal conversation.

"I suppose they got to sell if they've closed the place," Herb said. "I don't see that it makes any difference."

"It would if the new owners opened it up again," Jim said, and the conversation turned to the possibility of someone coming in and re-opening the plant.

Frank's coffee was done, so he dropped some change on the table and left. The day was fine and cold, but he decided to walk along Main Street to the post office. The only mail was flyers from the stores thirty minutes down the road. Local stores didn't put out flyers, they put a sign in the window. Too often these days it was Going out of business.

On impulse Frank walked into the library next door to the post office. He couldn't recall the last time he'd been in the library, maybe not since he'd left school.

"Good morning." The woman who spoke from behind the desk was Frank's age. She looked exotic for the town of Madison. Jennita, her name tag said.

"Good morning," Frank replied. "Do you have any books about rocks falling out of the sky?"

"Ah, you mean meteors." She smiled at Frank and led him to a section of bookshelf. "Just leave the books on the table when you're done. It lets me count what books have been read. If you have any other questions I'll be over at my desk."

"I thought Meteors were a car."

"Over in automotive history; next aisle." Jennita smiled again. "But they were named after the rocks."

Frank nodded and took out a book. He sat at the table and began to read. Jennita was right. He did want the rocks.

She had a nice smile. It warmed him like the second cup of Alice's coffee.

***

Frank got up the next morning and switched the still silent alarm off on the way out of the room. He glanced up at the clear blue sky. Snow tonight. He took extra time with the chores, talking with each of the animals and making sure they were healthy and content. Next he went over the old tractor, getting it ready for the night's work.

Frank found more than his usual contentment in doing work well as if he was aware of a connection to a much larger web. What he did with his life might not look important, but he had the feeling it was vital.

It was a bit later than usual when he headed into Alice's Coffee Shop, but the regulars were all there. There was a buzz of conversation already. They looked up and waved him to his seat.

Jim slid into the seat next to him.

"I was thinking 'bout what you said yesterday."

"You mean about shovels being on sale?" Frank gave Alice a nod as she filled his cup.

"About someone buying the plant and opening it up again."

"Yes?" Frank sipped from his cup and sighed.

"Why wait for someone to come into town and buy the place. They'd probably sell it again in a few years anyway." Frank nodded and sipped his coffee. The caffeine ran through his system. The bitterness of the coffee a balance to the sweetness of the energy it gave him.

"You listening?" Jim said.

"Yup," Frank said. "You and the guys want to buy the place yourselves."

"I was looking on the internet about co-ops and labour-owned factories... Hey, how did you know that?"

"You told me."

"Not yet I hadn't," Jim said, "I'd just got to the part about buyers coming and going."

"Except for a local buyer, but there isn't one person in town with that kind of pull, so we would have to make it a group effort."

"So you're in?"

"I think it's the only way to save our town," Frank said. "Glad you thought of it, Jim."

"I wouldn't have, 'cept for what you said. Rattled around in my head all night, and I woke up with the notion waiting for me to have my coffee." Jim leaned in close to Frank. "Mary likes the idea.

Things between us haven't been good since the plant closed. But she took to this like it was her that thought of it. Even if it don't work, t'will be worth it to see a smile on her face again."

Frank nodded. He knew the importance of a good smile.

"Whatever I can do, Jim," he said. "You just let me know."

"Frank's in!" There were cheers in the coffee shop and the others waved their cups in a toast.

"Maybe we can make this town what it once was again," Alice said as she refilled Frank's cup.

"Not what it once was, what it should be," Frank said. Alice gave him an odd look and went back to wiping the counter.

Frank finished his coffee and went outside. He decided with the sunshine that a walk would be nice. There wasn't much mail, but it was nice to chat with Jim's Mary who was the post mistress. He was glad to see her happy.

"I expect this office to be open on time," Bruce said as he came in. "I was here at nine o'clock and the doors were still locked."

"I'm sorry, Bruce," Mary said. "I got...delayed at home."

"Congratulations, Bruce," Frank said.

"What?"

"I was guessing the way that you were chewing out Mary that they'd gone and made you Post Master General."

Bruce turned red and opened his mouth, but no words came out. Mary behind him was hiding her grin behind a hand. He closed his mouth and glared at Frank before leaving.

"He's right though," Mary said. "I was late opening today."

"There's being right, and then there's being right the right way." Frank said, "Good to see Jim with some fire in his eyes again."

"You said it."

Frank decided to check the library again. The little vestibule at the entrance had a photograph of a Madison. Frank didn't know if it was a direct relation. There used to be a lot of Madisons. There used to be a lot of things in Madison that there weren't anymore.

"Hello," Jennita said.

"You were right about the meteor. Though when they land they're called meteorites."

Jennita's smiled sent crinkles dancing about her eyes.

"I'd forgotten about that."

"Funny how we use different words depending on where something is. You'd think that a thing was whatever it was no matter where it was."

"Words are more than labels: they talk about relationships between things too. Aren't you a farmer? A chicken on your farm is livestock, somewhere else it would be supper."

"The occasional chicken is supper on my farm too," Frank said.

"So what are you researching today?"

"I thought I'd do some reading on how to save a small town."

"Now, that is a big subject," Jennita said. She stood absolutely still for a long moment. Frank was sure that she was mentally scanning the bookshelves to decide where to send him. He found it fascinating.

"I think you should start with some recent history, then maybe some economics and perhaps some sociology. It will be a lot of reading."

"Won't be a bad thing to have a reason to come here every day."

Jennita's grin was more crinkly than the first one, and once again it felt like the warmth from the meteorite. She led him to the reading table and pulled a few books from the shelves.

"This should get you started. If you have any questions, just ask."

Frank sat down and picked up the first book. It was a history of Madison. He opened it and began reading.

Jennita interrupted Frank as he worked his way through the pile of books. He had developed a system of skimming through until a particular word or phrase caught his attention, then he would backtrack and read the interesting part.

"You must have been a go-getter at school," she said.

"Not really," Frank said. "Never liked reading." She laughed and looked at the pile of books that he had already gone through. Her laugh was as nice too. "I can read well enough, but I would always rather be doing than reading."

"I came over to ask if you wanted a cup of tea. I am making some for lunch."

"I don't know," Frank said. "I've never tried tea."

"The day is full of surprises. I find a fellow who dislikes reading surrounded by books, and he has never tried tea. You didn't visit any maiden aunts who forced tea with milk and sugar on you?"

"Never had any maiden aunts. The Madisons were always big on getting married. My Dad was immensely disappointed I didn't. I'll come and try your tea."

"OK then, just leave the books and come this way." The librarian led him to a plain door behind the desk. Frank was surprised that there weren't more books in the room. There were a few, but they were all about library science.

"Library science?"

"Don't get me started," Jennita said. "I could talk all day about how libraries are organized." She pulled out a couple of pottery mugs from a cupboard and set one in front of Frank. She poured it full of a dark amber liquid. Frank smelled it.

"It's Lapsang Souchong, a black china tea. It has a rather smoky flavour."

"I'm guessing you could talk awhile on tea too."

"Guilty as charged," Jennita smiled and took in a long breath over her mug. For a while they sat quietly. Frank sipped at the tea, and found it so utterly different from coffee that he took a while to decide if he liked it or not. He rather enjoyed the feeling. There weren't many truly new things in his life.

"So what brought you into the library all of a sudden?"

"A rock fell out of the sky and landed in a field next to me the other night while I was out on my tractor."

"Really?" Jennita's eyes widened. "That's amazing. Meteorites aren't really rare, but it is unusual for them to land near people."

"This was a big one. It took me most of the night to get it back to my shed."

"The big ones are rarer. I will bet that the observatory is looking for witnesses. They would love to see your meteorite."

"I don't know..." An echo of the warmth from the rock ran through him. "I don't think I'm ready to let the world come to my shed yet."

"Well, when you are ready we will let them know."

"Another new thing," Frank said.

"What's that?"

"Most folks I know would be trying to convince me to do the right thing, especially if it might mean money."

"I guess I'm not most folks."

"No, you're not." Frank said, "And I am appreciating it more every moment. Like this tea. It's subtle. It kind of sneaks up on you, then bang, you're thinking wow, this is great."

"Subtle? Lapsang?"

"Have you ever tried Alice's coffee?"

Jennita laughed, then took a sip from her own mug.

"That explains the books about meteors. I think the books about small towns are more obvious."

"I thought that if you had answers about falling rocks, you would have something about small towns."

"Only towns are a lot more complicated than rocks, even ones that fall from the sky."

"Yes." Frank sighed. "They certainly are."

"How are you getting along?"

"Slowly," he said, "I can see that this is going to take some time."

"I'll have to lay in more tea."

"I'd like that." A bell interrupted them.

"That's the door," she said getting up. "Go ahead and finish your tea."

Jennita left and her voice asking questions floated back through the door. He imagined her going still a moment and then leading the person to the shelf where they might find their answers. He took another long sip. Yup, this was most definitely growing on him.

***

When he arrived home he went out to the shed and uncovered the meteor.

"What do you think?" he said as he perched on the bucket of his tractor. "I think she's like her tea: subtle but full of something. I was never one for talking to the girls. That's why I live by myself with the animals and talk to rocks that fall from the sky." Frank looked out the window at the white of falling snow.

"Don't know what you did to me, but something is different. I never talked back to people before, but I seem to have lit a fire under Jim, and I certainly got Bruce mad enough at me. This librarian too, if I ever said two words to a girl without turning red I can't remember, and here I am drinking tea and chatting like old friends." He pulled the tarp back over the meteorite. "Whatever you did. I think I'm liking it."

Frank patted the rock and went to do his chores and have supper. It was going to be a long night on the tractor.

It was a long night, but Frank didn't feel as chilled as usual when the tractor chugged back into his shed. He climbed off the seat and stretched before patting the meteorite.

"Not a bad night, but we'll need a lot more snow to buy the plant. Then we need to figure out how to run it and how to sell the stuff we make. This co-op thing might save the town or finish it off. Now Jennita was saying that you were rare. I'm thinking rare might mean valuable. What do you think about me selling you to buy that plant?"

He adjusted the tarp carefully. "I think I need to wait for the right time."

After chores and clearing his own lane, Frank headed into town. The coffee shop was filled with regulars and some other townsfolk he recognized, but couldn't put a name to.

"Hey Frank." Jim waved him over to a table at the back. "We're having a meeting to talk about the plant."

"Here?"

"Why not? Coffee's hot."

Frank sat at the corner of the table.

"This is Herb's son, John. He's a real estate lawyer." Jim said

They shook hands.

"I've been telling the guys that from what I can find out, the company that bought the plant just walked away from it. That was cheaper than closing it down properly. The bank seized it while it tries to squeeze more money from the holding company."

"So we should be able to buy the place?"

"The title is still up in the air, while they may have seized it to cover outstanding debt, that doesn't give them clear title to sell."

"They sold Bob's farm quick enough."

"They were the only ones holding paper on the farm I would guess. Here there are probably half a dozen creditors arguing over the place."

"So it is complicated and impossible or complicated and doable?"

"I think it is worth putting out a proposal. No one will get richer letting the place rust."

"What about running it and finding buyers for the product?"

"I've been thinking about that Frank," Jim said. "We have someone in town who knows everything there is to know about that plant."

The door of the coffee shop slammed open and Frank heard his name called.

"Good morning Bruce." He said as he turned around.

"My drive wasn't cleared last night."

"You fired me."

"Well, I'm un-firing you. I need that drive clear."

Frank shrugged.

"Do you want it done now, or can I finish my coffee?"

Bruce looked ready to explode, then all the air went out of him and he dropped into an empty seat.

"It probably doesn't matter," he said, "I expect it's too late anyway."

Alice came and put a coffee in front of Bruce. He poured milk and sugar into it and drank it down.

"I'm trying to sell the place," Bruce said, "With the plant gone I don't have the money to pay the bills. Marg didn't want to move, but I wanted to be as good as the newcomers up on the hill."

"You are as good as them," Frank said, "Annoying at times, but that don't matter." He looked over at Jim who shrugged his shoulders. "Jim and the boys have been doing some thinking about the plant." Bruce looked up at him while Alice topped up his cup.

"What kind of thinking?"

"We've been talking about putting in a proposal to buy the plant and run it ourselves," Jim slid into the chair next to Bruce. "We need someone who knows how to run it."

"You want me to manage the plant for you?" Bruce shook his head, "You've worked for me for twenty years, why would you want to continue?"

"Because you kept the place running for twenty years." Jim looked around. "There's none of us could do it. You might be an ass at times, but you've mostly been a fair boss."

"I'll need to think about it. Talk to Marg. She was going on about moving south to be with her sister."

"That's all we can ask."

"I'll get to the drive today." Frank finished his coffee.

"Tonight will be soon enough." Bruce stood and left the shop.

"There's something I never thought I would see." Herb sat down where Bruce had been sitting. "Bruce acting all human. You're right though. We need him."

"Let's get some numbers put together and we can start roughing out a proposal. We don't want the bank selling it for salvage before we get our bid in." John dragged the men back to their table at the rear.

Alice sat down across from Frank. Alice had never sat down in her own restaurant in all the years he had known her.

"What you said about us working to become what we should be. What did you mean by that?"

"I don't rightly know," Frank admitted. "I don't think we can go back to what we were. So, I guess we have to go forward."

"That's what I thought." Alice smiled and stood up again. "If I weren't married, I'd kiss you. You're a genius Frank."

Frank sat and listened to the buzz in the shop for a while, then went to the library. Jennita waved at him as he came in, then went back to talking to the young men who were standing by her desk. He went back to the table and pulled out a book. He wasn't reading long before he heard Jennita's voice raised.

When Frank ambled out of the shelves he found the young men had cornered her against the desk. One of them looked to be grabbing her arm. The kind of things coming of the kid's mouth made him clench his teeth.

"Excuse me, Miss," he said in his best farmer voice, "I'm having some trouble finding a book."

"There are lots of books, old man, go pick one," the young man said.

"They aren't all the right books."

"What does it matter? Can you read anyway?"

"Better than you, I figure."

"What?"

"I can read the sign asking folks to be quiet in the library."

The young man waited a fraction of a second too long to answer and his friends nudged him then pulled him outside.

"No fun in here. This place is so dead."

Jennita slumped against the desk.

"Thanks, they've been in before and been rude, but nothing like this."

"My name's Frank."

Jennita looked at him.

"I know, Mary told me."

"Figured, but I thought I should introduce myself before taking the liberty of giving you advice."

"Ah, and what would the advice be?"

"I think we should have a cup of your tea, and you can tell me all about it until you stop shaking."

"That," Jennita said, "sounds like excellent advice."

***

In Jennita's office Frank put kettle on to boil and rinsed out the teapot. He didn't say anything until he had completed the last of her whispered instructions and put the full mug in her hands. Just the warmth of the ceramic seemed to steady her. She breathed in the fumes of the brew.

"They're just bored kids from the new development." Jennita said.

"Not just kids," Frank said, "I heard a car driving away."

"They're still kids," she said, "They've never had to grow up. Everything they want is handed to them."

"Seems like an awful way to live."

"Frank, you keep surprising me. Most people would like nothing better than to have everything handed to them on a platter."

"Not you."

"No, not me either." She took another deep breath and a tiny sip. "Strong, just like you."

"Sorry, it's the first time I made tea."

"I'm not complaining. I like my tea strong," She looked at him and smiled faintly. "Like my men strong too." Frank took a careful sip of tea. It was strong, and got better with each sip.

"I lived in a city with my husband and kids. I worked at the central library and never thought how lucky I was to be living my life. Not until there was an accident at Pete's work. The insurance was generous, but money didn't replace the feeling of a warm body on the other side of the bed nor change the fact there were too many things I never told him. I didn't need to go back to work, so I stayed home and tried to tell my kids all the things that I never told Pete." She got up to put her cup in the sink, and stood for a bit with her back to Frank.

"I'm not sure they understood. First one, then the other went off to school, fell in love, made their own way. After my youngest's wedding I gave them the keys to the house and took the first librarian's job that I found. Here in Madison I've remade myself. I am Jennita the librarian, not Pete's widow. I walk in and see all the books, and know this is where I am supposed to be. Here. Now." Jennita turned around to face Frank again.

"You are the first person since Pete died that has made me think that there might be a person I am supposed to be with." Her hands knotted together.

"I liked your smile the first time I saw it," Frank said, "It grew on me. Like Alice's coffee at the shop or this Lapsang tea. I never could talk to the girls, but you make me feel like I've known you for years - comfortable."

"So what now Frank?" Jennita sat across from him again.

"I'd take you to lunch at Alice's, only she'd have us engaged before we got to the pie."

Jennita laughed, the sound of it was like bells ringing inside of Frank. He grinned at this woman who had suddenly become very important to him.

She reached across the table and took his hand.

"Thanks, for being there, Frank. Those boys do scare me at times."

"Let me think what I can do. They shouldn't be able to treat people like that."

"I don't think talking to them will change anything."

"No, I don't suppose it would."

The bell indicated someone coming into the library. Jennita took a deep breath and stood up. Frank stood up too.

"Do you want me to come with you?"

"No, I need to face this myself, but thank you." She kissed him lightly on the lips and went out to see who had come in.

Frank stood there for a long moment with a wide grin on his face. He finally sat down and finished his tea deep in thought, yet still keeping his ears open to hear if Jennita needed him. The question of how to keep the library safe kept getting mixed up with the question of how to spend more time with the librarian. When his tea was done, he slipped out and back to his books, but he found it harder and harder to concentrate.

At closing time, she came by.

"Don't you have chores to do?" she asked. "I love having you here, but not if it is taking you away from something you need to be doing."

"I check on the animals in the evening. Plenty of time yet." He helped her carry the books to the desk. "I have a idea about those boys. I'll tell you tomorrow."

He looked at Jennita, then did the scariest thing he had done in a very long time. He leaned over and kissed her on the lips.

"Good night, Jennita."

"Good night, Frank." She smiled at him and waved as she locked the door behind him.

The weather appeared to be taking its cue from the warmth in his heart. Frank watched the drifts that he had been driving through with the tractor vanish. As much as he liked the extra income from the driveway work, he appreciated the extra time to spend with his animals thinking.

He couldn't remember ever spending so much time thinking. Thinking about economics, thinking about his friends and neighbours, thinking about Jennita. To be truthful, most of the thinking was about Jennita. Where he'd always had to struggle to think of what to say to girls when he was young, now the words flowed effortlessly.

He went through his evening chores in a fog of bemused happiness. The animals were quiet so it wasn't too long before he was sitting in the shed looking at the meteorite.

"I have some ideas about the library," he said as he leaned back against the big tractor tire. "But I'm going to need to ask for some help. I think Jim is busy enough with this business with the plant, so I am going to ask Alice. She knows everybody. If she thinks it will work, then it will work."

Frank stood and stretched.

"So unless you disagree, I will talk to Alice tomorrow." He smiled crookedly. "The cows thought it was a good idea too. If I wasn't so happy right now, I'd be concerned about me. But for some reason this feels right."

He closed and locked the door to the shed and went to the house for the night.

***

Next day after chores he drove into town.

"How's it going?" he asked Jim as he entered the shop. His friend was sitting at the back table surrounded by papers and folders. Herb and his son were sitting beside him and helping him fill out forms.

"How much is the farm worth?" Jim asked, "We need another million to put together a decent offer. I was hoping that each of the two hundred some employees would be able to come up with ten thousand each, but lots of them are already maxed out."

"I'll talk to the bank, but I doubt there is that much in the farm."

Jim nodded. "We're close, but I want a really solid proposal. John says we might have a week. He has heard some rumbles about an offshore company buying the place."

"I'll stop in today and talk to Jenkins. He should be able to give me a ball park figure anyway. Has Bruce decided yet?"

"He hasn't talked to me yet, but Marg was talking to Mary at the post office and she thinks it is a great idea."

"Great." Frank went over and sat at the counter. Alice wasn't there. A new girl with black lipstick and a ring in her bottom lip poured his coffee for him.

"Hi, where's Alice this morning?" He peered at the girl's name tag. "Alixxa."

"She's at a meeting. Aunt Alice told me I could work here for a while."

Frank took a sip of the coffee and sighed.

"If you make coffee like this, you can work here all you want."

The girl laughed and Frank caught a glimpse of metal in the girl's mouth.

"Maybe you can help me out." She looked around the shop and shrugged.

"What do you need?"

"I was at the library and some young men came in were being rude. They scared the librarian. Can you think why they would do that?"

"Just because I have metal in me, you think I'm a punk?"

"No, no. You're younger and have a different background than me. I wanted to hear your thoughts."

"Really?"

"Really."

She wandered through the shop pouring coffee and Frank sipped at his. It was still coffee, but it was nothing like what Alice usually served. He liked it.

"I think," Alixxa said when she came back to refill his cup, "that they're bored." She put a new pot of coffee on to perk. "Punks like that have too much time on their hands and not enough to do that matters. We had them at home too. Kids who just didn't seem to know how to give a sh... I mean they didn't care about anything. I don't think they knew how to care. Mom was afraid I was turning into one. So, she shipped me off to Aunt Alice to get straightened out."

"You don't think you need straightening."

"Nah, I'm just trying things on. Today, this is who I am. Tomorrow?" She shrugged. "Who knows?"

"Thanks Alixxa," Frank said.

She nodded and went back to wiping counters.

Frank finished his coffee and walked over to the bank. Jenkins was talking to a man in a suit who was looking annoyed. They finished their conversation when the man waved his hands in the air and walked out of the bank.

"How can I help you Frank?"

"You know about the proposal?"

"You want to stay away from that Frank." Jenkins said. "You can lose your shirt real easy with that."

"How much could I safely put in?"

"Let me think." Jenkins stared up at the ceiling for a long moment, "You aren't carrying a lot of mortgage, so probably two-fifty, even three hundred. Like I said it's risky. You could lose the farm if it goes wrong." He leaned against the desk. "You might be better selling some land to the right people. There are developers who are desperate for places to build."

"Like the man you were talking to?"

Jenkins shook his head. "He wanted me to point him toward someone who was close to losing everything. I told him it wasn't ethical. He told me ethics has no place in business."

"Remind me never to do business with him."

"He'd buy one of your acreages in a minute."

"My dad would spin in his grave if I sold good farm land to build houses for rich people."

"Sell the bad stuff then. They don't care. They'll bulldoze everything anyway."

"Thanks for the help, Jenkins."

"I don't know if I was a help or not," he said. "Time will tell."

Frank walked toward the post office and saw Alice on the street.

"Hey Alice," he called, "how'd your meeting go?"

"Good and bad," she said. "We're putting a local business association together. Everyone likes the idea, but no one knows what to do with it."

"It will come."

"I hope so, and soon. There are a lot of us that are just scraping by. We can't compete with the big malls down the road."

"Don't try. What I was reading at the library said that service and uniqueness are what sell."

"I heard you been spending considerable time at the library."

Frank felt his face turning red.

"She's a real nice woman, Frank." She poked him in the chest. "And you're a nice man. You'd be good for each other."

"That's sort of why I wanted to talk to you," Frank told her about the incident the day before. She nodded. "I was thinking if we had more people in the library, they wouldn't think they could get away with that kind of behaviour."

"So you want me to get more people going to the library?"

"Partly, but people need a reason. Maybe your business association will have some ideas."

"More problems. As if I didn't have enough already. You met my sister's kid?"

"Alixxa?" Frank said, "She seems nice enough. She makes good coffee."

"And I don't?"

"Alice, you make great coffee, but it's small town coffee. Alixxa does something different and it is good too."

"So what am I supposed to do with her. The shop is barely covering cost with just me at the counter."

"Maybe she will have some ideas."

"She certainly has lots of opinions."

"Does it hurt to ask?"

"Frank, whatever that librarian is doing to you, I approve. Bring her by for lunch some day." Alice went off toward her shop and Frank walked on down to the library to spend another day reading and soaking in Jennita's presence.

   ***

The weather continued to warm through the next weeks. Jim was frantically trying to put his offer on the table. He and John finally submitted a preliminary proposal. According to Jim, Jenkins had sighed and shook his head, but promised to pass it along to his superiors.

Frank alternated between sitting at Alice's shop and drinking her coffee and sitting at the library and drinking tea. Jennita didn't have as much time as she once had for drinking tea. Suddenly groups appeared and wanted to meet in the library. Jennita was delighted even as it made her busier.

It started with a Story Time group organized by one of Alice's young friends. The first day there were only three mothers and four children, but a woman from the new development noticed the group while she was checking out some books and brought her child. Soon the children's section was filled each Tuesday and Thursday morning. The mothers and the occasional father found that the stories were universal. For the first time old times and newcomers were talking about more than the weather.

A woman from the development started the knitting circle, but soon, every Wednesday the reading room filled with woman clicking away on knitting needles. Conversation began with discussion around patterns, but soon meandered into broad and fruitful paths. More connections were built between old and new.

Friday was the book club. Jennita would pull out the newest books and they would read and discuss them.

The library became the start of a gradual change in the town. Frank saw part of it in the hardware store when the knitting woman came in. Usually the newcomers would drive to the big stores for what they wanted.

"Hello," she called, "I'd like to buy some paint."

"Certainly," Joe said, "what room are you painting?"

"The kitchen."

"Ah, you'll want an eggshell, maybe even a semi-gloss if you are painting around the stove."

"Why?"

"Easier to clean. Any grease from cooking will wipe off much easier."

'What colours do you carry?"

"I can mix just about anthing you like."

"I was thinking a brick colour for behind the counter, and something lighter for the rest of the kitchen."

"What colour are your cabinets?"

"Dark oak."

"That should be nice, but you might want an accent to brighten it up." He pulled out some paint chips and passed them to her. "Have a look at these."

"Hmmm," she said. "I'm not sure."

"How about I mix up a couple of samples and you put them on the wall. Leave them for a day or two and see which ones you like."

"You can do that?"

"Sure thing...."

Frank took his bag of nails to the counter and weighed them. He wrote the weight on a paper and left it and some money on the counter. He waved at Joe, who waved back while he was showing the woman different kinds of paint brushes.

At Alice's he found a seat at the counter. A man in a blue suit sat beside him stirring his coffee.

"Hello Frank," Alice said as she poured his coffee, then she rushed off to take another order.

"Is the coffee always like this?" the man in the suit asked.

"Pretty much," Frank said.

"It's awfully strong."

"It grows on you."

"Hmmmm." The man added another spoonful of sugar and sipped. He shuddered and took another sip. By the bottom of the cup he wasn't shuddering, but he didn't ask for a refill.

Alixxa came by after the man left.

"Another happy customer." she poked at the sludge at the bottom of the cup. "I bet he wouldn't look like he was being poisoned if I had made the coffee."

"I heard that!" Alice said. "I make the best coffee in these parts. Isn't that right Frank?"

"Your coffee is just fine for me, Alice, but that fellow was struggling with it. Maybe it's the suit."

"Let me make coffee for the new people, please," Alixxa begged. "What can it hurt?"

"OK, OK," Alice said. "Why couldn't you want to do dishes?" She went off scrubbing counters.

Alixxa sighed.

"I don't want to upset her, but these guys aren't ready for my Aunt's brew."

"You may be right, but take it easy on her. This shop is all she has left."

"She has me."

"She doesn't know the value of that yet."

Frank finished his coffee and walked down toward the library. If the knitting group was done, Jennita might have a little time to talk.

Alice's Coffee Shop wasn't the only place that was suddenly a lot busier. Frank found a crowd of people wandering through the library as the knitters packed up. Jennita was explaining something to a young man with several earrings and a spike sticking out of his eyebrow. She waved at Frank and pointed to her office. He waved back and started the process of brewing tea. He had taken to using a random scoop from one of her many tins and seeing if she could identify the tea.

Today he used something called Keemun China Black.

Jennita came in with the young man as he was setting out the mugs. Frank picked another mug off the shelf and set it down.

"This is Sergio," she said. "The head office decided with the numbers we were generating that I needed an assistant. Sergio, this is Frank, a big supporter of the library and a very dear friend."

"Hi Frank," Sergio said and shook hands. "What do you like to read?"

"Mostly whatever is in front of me," Frank said. "Right now that seems to be cooperatives and micro-economics."

"Wow! I'm impressed," he sipped at the tea, "I am usually a coffee drinker, but Jennita is trying to convert me."

"You'll want to try the coffee at Alice's, but get Alixxa to pour you her coffee first. Alice's brew is unique and powerful."

"I'll go have lunch there. It will give you and Jennita a bit of time to talk."

They finished their tea accompanied by polite conversation, then Sergio rinsed out his mug and sauntered out of the office.

"I think he's going to be good for the library. He's a lot better at the internet stuff than I am, and he reads the oddest selection of books. I watched him pick a book off the shelf and read a page at random."

"There seems to be lots of stuff happening these days, I don't know how people are keeping up with all the change."

"It's exciting right now, later it will be terrifying."

Frank finished his tea and went back out into the main part of the library. He saw Sergio talking to the aggressive youngster who had scared Jennita. The man in the suit who stood behind him tapping his foot Frank recognized from the bank. To his surprise the man came over to him.

"DeLorne, of DeLorne and Associates," he said. "I'm looking at some land to develop and I am told that you own the land with the old gravel pit to the west of town."

"That would be me," Frank said.

"Come in and talk to me about it. I will get you top dollar for it."

"I don't know that I want to sell."

"Don't see why not. Make some money from a useless piece of land."

"The deer like it there."

"Deer." The man barked what Frank thought was laughter and handed him a card. "Get a move on Greg," he called, and went out the door. The young man glared at his father's back then stalked out after him.

Frank looked at the card for a minute then went out of the library. He headed down the street to the bank.

He found Jenkins in his office doing paperwork.

"What can I do for you Frank? I only have a minute though, so if it is complicated I will have to book an appointment for you."

"That old acreage with the gravel pit," Frank said, "How much would it be worth if it was developed?"

"You aren't thinking of selling to that shark in a business suit are you?"

"Nope, but if that land is worth a chunk of money as a potential development, doesn't that give me some more leverage to raise some money?"

"Hmm, you might be right, but you would need a hard offer or re-zoning to make it work. I'd go for the re-zoning though. Once that man talks offers he isn't going to let it go."

"I'll ask Herb, he's on the Council. He'd know what I need to do." Jenkins shrugged and went back to his papers and Frank went to find Herb.

Herb dragged him over to the town office and had the clerk look up the acreage.

"It looks like DeLorne has been doing his research. That is in an area that is already allotted for future growth, so a zoning change won't be hard. The biggest problem is going to be dealing with how ticked off he will be that you didn't sell to him."

"He does seem eager."

"Whatever he is offering you isn't enough. There are lots of other considerations, but acreage like that is worth a small fortune."

"Thanks Herb." Frank looked at the papers. "How about I ask for preliminary approval for the zone change. That might be enough to leverage the bank, but not so rushed that it will raise eyebrows."

"Good idea."

Frank left them the filled-out forms and walked back to his truck. He drove out to the old pit and parked. He got out of the truck and walked back off the road. There were deer tracks, raccoon too.

"Sorry folks, but you may have to move."

The crunch of gravel announced another person arriving.

"Glad you see it my way," DeLorne came up behind Frank. "I'll put some two acre lots around the center here. Maybe a pond. Put some smaller places farther back. Make this a real draw for the up and coming. Come by the office. I'll have the girls do up the papers." He looked at his watch and walked back to his car. With spinning tires and flying gravel he sped off down the road.

"You know," Frank said to the gravel pit, "I really don't like him."

***

The trickle of changes in Madison became a flood. Stores that had been closed for years were suddenly opening as antique shops or boutiques selling very expensive items useless for anything but decoration. Frank no longer knew every person he met on Main St. When he did meet someone, they had to stand to one side to let the flow of strangers pass.

Frank walked into the newly expanded Alice's Coffee shop.

"I don't know my own town anymore," Jim said as Frank sat signing papers. "Even Alice's is changing." The table where they sat was in the store next door to the Coffee Shop. Alice had bought it and moved most of the furniture there while her husband tore out and redecorated the original shop. Alixxa served coffee from a make-shift counter at the back.

"I know, Jim." Frank pushed the papers over to his friend. "It's like the gravel pit, get the council to say it is one thing instead of another and suddenly it's worth more than a winning lottery ticket."

"I hope this is enough. Jenkins told me there's an off-shore group trying to buy the plant. If they get it, who knows what they will do with it?" He waved his mug at Alixxa.

"You know I tell all the other customers they have to come to the counter," she said as she filled his cup. "I'd never have thought chaos would be so good for business. Sergio loaned me a cappuccino maker to try out, and all these folks pour in the door." She waved at someone standing by the counter and went back to work.

The door crashed open and Greg, who had started the trouble at the library walked in with his friends.

"What do I need to do to get some service here?" he shouted.

"Wait in line like everyone else," Alixxa said.

He walked up to the counter and sneered at her.

"Do you know what I do to little girls like you?"

"You pay me for your coffee, just like everyone else."

"My Dad could buy a dozen places like this."

"Well run home and ask him for one, then you won't need to bother me."

He reached over and grabbed her arm. In seconds Frank stood on one side of him while Jim loomed over him on the other.

"Time to leave," Frank said. The young man looked at him and sneered some more. His friends watched from their seats.

"What are you going to do? If my father doesn't own you yet, he will soon enough."

"Your father can't own anybody that won't sell himself."

"You're selling that land to him aren't you? He owns you."

"You're not only a very rude young man, but you're pretty stupid too," Frank looked him in the eye and stepped closer. "If I am indeed one of your father's associates, he wouldn't appreciate you insulting me. If I'm not one of his associates, he'll be angry that you are discussing his business with me."

"So?"

"So, regardless of who your father is, you're just a small-time bully trying to throw your daddy's weight around. Do you really think I haven't seen plenty of your kind before?" He reached over and picked up a cup of coffee and put it in the boy's hand. "Here's your coffee, now run to daddy, and tell him that Frank Madison is not selling his land. Not to him, not to anyone associated with him."

The boy tossed the coffee on the floor and stormed out of the shop. One of his friends shrugged apologetically before he followed. Jim stepped around the counter and came back out with the mop and cleaned up the mess. Before he finished someone stepped up to the counter to order.

Frank left the shop with his gut churning from his anger. There were some things about the new Madison that he didn't like. The DeLorne men was a fair number of them. By the time he reached the library he had managed to get himself back to an equilibrium.

Jennita had a half dozen people waiting to talk to her. Sergio was helping a couple of kids with the computer. Frank contented himself with a wave as he went to the reading area and picked out a book.

The book finished the work of calming him. Frank didn't remember much of what he read, but he wasn't worried about that today. He didn't think the answers he was looking for were going to be found in print.

He sighed and put it down. Jennita's line was still long, but different people, so he waved again and went out onto the street.

DeLorne met him.

"What do you mean you aren't selling?" he said. "We had an agreement."

"No," Frank said, "we didn't. You never asked if I was selling, You decided you were buying."

"You had it re-zoned."

"I had my reasons."

"What is it? Do you want more money?" DeLorne's face was getting red.

"Don't want any amount of your money."

"Nobody messes with me!" He pushed Frank with his finger. "You are nothing. Nothing!"

"Pardon me, Mr. Madison," the Sheriff interrupted DeLorne. "Is this gentleman bothering you?"

"He's just leaving, Sheriff."

"This isn't over, Madison." DeLorne gave him a parting glare and left.

"He's been buying land all over the district," the Sheriff said. "There are some folks who are desperate enough to sell at any price. I don't think he's made anyone but himself rich yet."

Frank nodded. He went to his truck and drove out to the farm. Even on the back roads, the traffic was heavier. At his farm, he checked on the livestock. Caring for the animals gave him a calm that even reading couldn't.

The town had dealt with people like DeLorne before. His grandfather had been like that. Frank's father had no interest in anything but farming and his father had never forgiven him for it. By the time Frank had been old enough to remember, his grandfather was dead. Only his father's bitter stories and an over-sized headstone remained of the old man's ambitions.

When the chores were done, he went out the shed and uncovered the meteor.

"I should have known that there would be the bad with the good," Frank said. "That's the way of it, isn't it?" He sat on the stone and patted it. "I suppose I'll muddle by like I usually do. Life will go on." He left the meteor uncovered and went to cook his supper.

After supper Frank poked through some of the boxes of stuff that his parents had left in the attic rooms. It took him a while to find the property deeds he was looking for, but he didn't mind. It had been a long time since he had looked at the pictures that were all he had left of his parents.

The sound of breaking glass brought him downstairs. He saw a strange car in the drive and heard more destruction from the shed. Frank called the Sheriff's office. The girl told him to stay in the house, but that was Franks livelihood in the shed, and he didn't want to think about what would happen if the invaders got into the barn.

They didn't hear him come through the door. Frank wasn't surprised to see the young DeLorne and his two hangers on. They had smashed all the windows in the shed and were trying to break the tractor windshield.

"The Sheriff's coming." Frank said. "I'd appreciate you leaving now." He used the same voice he used when an animal was upset and dangerous.

The young man who had shrugged in the coffee shop pulled on the DeLorne kid's arm.

"Come on, Greg," he said. "We need to get out of here."

Greg pushed him away.

"I'm not afraid of some punk sheriff." He pulled a pistol out of his pocket and shot a hole in the tractor's windshield. "I'm not afraid of anyone." He pointed the gun at his friend.

"Easy," Frank said, still speaking like they were spooked animals.

The gun swung around until it was pointed at him.

"Why do you have a big fricking rock in here?"

"It's a meteorite," Frank said. "I haven't decided what to do with it yet."

Greg laughed and waves of alcohol hit Frank's face.

"You mean like in those dumb movies? Does it give you super powers?" He pulled the trigger and a burning pain ran through Frank's shoulder.

"I guess not." He swaggered over to Frank who leaned against the tractor with his hand on his shoulder.

"Let me tell you a secret." He waved the gun in Frank's face and breathed more alcohol at him. "Pay attention old man!" He grabbed Frank and pushed him over onto the meteorite.

"Nobody messes with the DeLorne's"

Siren announced the Sheriff's approach. The other two young men were frantic, but neither one wanted to face the gun. Finally, they ran out the door.

"Chicken, both of them, but then you know all about chicken." He made clucking noises at Frank. The sirens wailed to a stop, but Greg paid no attention.

"FREEZE!" The Sheriff's bellow got the kid's attention. He turned to aim the gun at the Sheriff. Frank looked at the kid. The kid is a jerk and a bully, but he doesn't deserve to die. He lunged up and grabbed the kid's arm and wrenched the gun away and threw it into a corner. Greg swung at him and clipped his face. Frank threw the kid toward the Sheriff who caught him and had him on the ground in seconds.

The pain in Frank's shoulder suddenly got worse and he opened his mouth to say something, but nothing came out. He fell back on the meteorite his blood running out across the stone. He felt some of the same connection he had the first time he touched it. There was an answer in there, but he couldn't grasp it. The Sheriff shouted into his radio, but it was a distant echo.

The meteorite was pulled Frank into itself.
***

It was cold inside the stone, and dark.

Frank floated in space. The heat of the sun burned his face and feel the bitter cold his back. The hard, unwinking stars stood aloof. Space, as its name suggested was empty. Frank was alone.

The longer Frank was in space the harder it became for him to get a sense of place and speed. At one moment hurtled along, the next he was at a dead stop. It was disconcerting, so he closed his eyes and tried to figure out what was going on. There was nothing. No breath of wind, no pull of gravity hinted at how he related to the universe.

He opened his eyes and looked at the stars again. *They were lucky, they knew their place.* He was just a chunk of rock, alone in space.

He didn't know how long he was in space before he began to hear the music. The music started as chords. Low notes made his teeth itch while high notes were a bare whisper in the aether.

The chords shifted and changed, now major, now minor, now a dominant seven or augmented fourth. Dissonances had him ready to scream and then resolutions which brought him to tears. The more he listened the easier it became to discern, not a melody, but a direction to the music. He felt with all his being that the music was taking him somewhere. His speed of travel or time in space was only relevant in relationship to the great Song.

Yet it in the midst of the wonder and beauty of the Song, something was missing. Even with the breadth of the chords there was another note that he needed to hear. Tentatively, fearfully, Frank hummed the note.

As soon as he hummed that note, the space around him changed. He was part of the great Dance, a singer in the great Song. What was empty became full. Frank traveled through music more glorious than he could bear. The stars were not far off and aloof, but his family. Their song accompanied him as his made them richer. He sang hope with a nebula, and sorrow with a quasar.

Now, not only was space filled with the vast fellowship of creation, but his journey had a destination. A tiny blue planet circled a small yellow star. Frank would add himself to that planet's song. He would give up his note to make the planet's note richer and more vibrant.

As he entered the atmosphere the heat increased. His outer skin melted and reformed. Frank's song became an ecstasy of joy, of peace, of purpose. He crashed into the earth and married himself to the planet's fate.

The warmth of his love radiated out into his surroundings, he offered his part of the Song to whoever listened. And someone was listening, unaware, unknowing. Frank touched him and something of the great Song crossed between. They talked and sat in communion not seeking answers, but to be.

Then an answer was needed, and Frank tried to put the vastness of the Dance, the hugeness of the Song into words. Once the connection reformed words became unnecessary. Frank belonged. He was not alone.

But words were necessary. Others needed to hear, to dance. Frank struggled to speak. Somehow he must fit all that was, into a breath of sound and air.

Then someone touched him and called him to himself.

***

"Frank, Frank," the voice said, and he could hear the tears. "Frank, you can't leave me now. Please come back." A bolt of light went through him and anchored his feet to the earth and sent his heart soaring.

He took a breath and opened his eyes.

Frank was lying in a hospital bed surrounded by flowers, balloons and cards, but even the clouds of well wishes couldn't distract him from Jennita who sat beside him holding his hand tightly.

"He's awake!" she shouted, and a nurse came in to take his pulse. She nodded in satisfaction.

"You can have small sips of water for now. Your throat will be dry, but don't overdo it." Frank thought she was somewhat cool and aloof until she gave Jennita's shoulder a squeeze on the way out.

He tried to say something, but his voice refused to work.

"Shh," Jennita said, "don't talk," she held the cup of water for him to sip "It isn't tea, but it will do." She pushed tears away from her eyes. "Here I am being all foolish, I was looking at you in the bed and started thinking about Pete."

Frank squeezed her hand.

"I suppose you're right. Even here in Madison, there is a part of me that is Pete's widow." She smiled through the tears. "But isn't the most important part, not by a long shot."

Half way through squeezing her hand again Frank fell asleep.

The next time he woke the room was dark and Jennita was curled up sleeping in the chair. He managed to reach the water and take a sip. That wore him out so he closed his eyes and went back to sleep.

The nurse woke him in the morning taking his pulse and blood pressure. She helped him to the washroom and back.

"You're doing great," the nurse said. "You will be heading home in no time."

Frank poked at the huge bandage that covered his shoulder. He felt a dull ache.

"The bullet went right through, but it nicked an artery. The surgeon did some neat work to get it all sewn up. I doubt you will have any permanent problems with the shoulder." She cranked up the bed so he was mostly sitting.

Jennita came in carrying two steaming cups.

"I remember that you like coffee first in the morning. Alixxa sent you her best." Frank reached for the cup.

"Go ahead and enjoy it." the nurse said.

He peeled back the lid and sipped at the coffee. Warmth and strength flowed through him.

"Thanks," he said.

"Hey," Jennita said, "You talk."

"Never mind modern medicine, coffee is the real miracle drug." *Not as powerful as you.*

"Mmm." Jennita sipped at her cup. "It is robust, but I still like my tea."

"Good, because I like the tea too. Everything in its place." He contented himself with drinking in Jennita's presence. There'd be time for words later.

"Hey folks," Jim said as he carried in a couple of steaming cups. "Alice figured I'd be here in time to bring a refill." He handed one to Frank, Jennita waved the second cup off.

"I think I should take this coffee thing slowly," she said.

Jim chuckled, pulled over a chair and sat down.

"How are you doing?"

"I'm told that I'm doing just fine," Frank said. "I'm inclined to believe it."

"Good, good." Jim took a long sip of the coffee and sighed. "The guys are taking turns doing chores at your place, so don't you worry about the animals. Herb's got a crew cleaning up the shed and fixing the glass." He looked at Frank over his cup. "Everyone is curious about that rock you have sitting there."

"It's a meteor," Frank tried to sit up straighter and winced. Jennita adjusted the bed for him. "Actually a meteorite."

"You mean that chunk fell out of the sky?"

"Yup," Frank said and told him the story of how he found it. "I did some research on those rocks. One of the things I learned was that they are valuable."

"That rock?"

"A fellow found one in his field, weighed about fifteen pounds. They figured it was worth almost half a million."

Jim choked on his coffee. Jennita thumped his back until he could talk.

"How much does that thing weigh?"

"I don't really know. A lot," Frank said with a shrug. "It doesn't matter. I don't figure on selling it. It wouldn't be right."

Jim shook his head.

"I have some other news for you," he said. "Herb's boy and I were trying to pitch the numbers to the board of the bank. Jenkins was sympathetic, but his bosses were inclined to sell to this offshore group that DeLorne was pushing. Every time we said something he had some number that was bigger or smaller than ours. He sat there smug as anything and watched us drown. No, worse, he was pushing our heads under. I knew that we were all going to lose our shirts and that the bastard was going to end up owning all of us.

"The bank folks were about going to kick us out and sign with DeLorne's group when the Sheriff busted in and damned if he didn't arrest DeLorne right there for conspiracy to commit murder. John just casually laid the idea on them that if that was the kind of person these offshore people hired to represent them, what would they do the bank? They couldn't sign that offer fast enough.

"So now we own the plant. Bruce already has been feeling out the markets, and we can supply parts for windmills without having to completely retool the plant." Jim shrugged, "Who knew? Windmills. We have a crew over there getting the place in shape. We'll be up and running by the end of the month."

"So DeLorne's boy did us a favour."

"What?"

"If he hadn't gone after me, it might have worked out different. Just goes to show, everyone has a place. We may not like it, but that's the way it works."

"Are you sure that rock didn't land on your head?" Jim laughed. "You never talked like that before."

Frank lay back again.

"Oops, I've got to move," Jim said. "I'm meeting Herb and John to sign more papers. It's a good thing that punk didn't shoot your right shoulder 'cause you have your share to sign too."

He waved at Jennita and left.

Frank closed his eyes for a few moments and felt Jennita's hand in his just before he fell asleep again.

He woke up when he heard the Sheriff's voice in the room.

"...yes, but he's out on bail. His kid is still in the cells. He was making threats all over the place. When he told the judge he would hunt her down she decided that he could wait in jail for trial. Funny thing, I'd expect a guy like DeLorne to be crying harassment and false arrest. Instead he's almost humble. His wife's the one who owns that new wool shop in town. She just stood behind him and never said a word, but I'm thinking she has something to do with his new attitude."

"DeLorne isn't bad," Frank said. "He's just short sighted. I think his eyes got opened to the cost of the way he does business."

126

"Glad to see you're awake, Frank," the Sheriff said. "I don't want to tire you too much, but if you're up to making a statement...."

Frank went through the events of the shooting with the Sheriff, by the time he finished, he was exhausted. He woke twice in the night. Jennita sleeping in the chair beside him.

The next day the doctor told him he could go home as long as he promised not to do any heavy work. Jennita drove him back to the farm. Bob was finishing chores as they pulled in. He waved and drove off.

Frank settled in his chair and heaved a big sigh.

"It's good to be home."

***

"I'll put some supper together." Jennita went into the kitchen and Frank listened to her poking around finding things. He thought about getting up and helping her, but the chair was comfortable and he didn't feel like moving.

They walked through the barn after supper and Frank introduced her to the animals. Jennita petted each one of them.

She gave him a kiss at the door and told him she would come by in the morning.

Frank woke in the middle of the night. His eyes refused to close, so he put on his robe and wandered out to the shed. True to Jim's promise all the mess had been cleaned up. Someone had even polished the meteorite.

"I'm thinking I need to thank you," Frank said. "Don't know that any of this would have happened if you hadn't happened along." He sat on the rock and thought for a while.

"I think it is time I shared you with some more people," he said finally. "I've an idea that you'll like it where I have a mind to put you." Frank was tired now, so he walked back to the house and made a brief detour to the parlour that he almost never used. It only took him a moment to find what he was looking for. Then he went to bed.

In the morning the sounds and smells of cooking woke him. Frank wrapped his robe around him and went out to greet his visitors. Jennita had brought Alixxa with her.

"I don't know how to make coffee," Jennita said. "Alice loaned me Alixxa as long as I had her back for the lunch crowd." Alixxa waved from where she was pouring coffee into one of Frank's chipped mugs.

They ate breakfast in companionable silence. After struggling into his clothes, Frank went out to watch Bob doing the chores. They sat on the porch and finished off the pot of coffee. Bob headed off to the plant and Frank went into town with Jennita and Alixxa.

The coffee shop was full, but people, both strangers and friends welcomed Frank and made space for him to sit. Alice came over and just looked at him.

"This place just wouldn't be the same without you," she said. "I'm glad you're OK."

"I'm thinking we'll have the lunch special, Alice." Frank said. "I've been pining for your good food."

"Two specials, coming right up," Alice said she walked through the plastic sheet that still divided the two rooms and called the order to the kitchen.

"I don't mean anything bad about your cooking," Frank whispered to Jennita as he took her hand. Jennita refused to let go, so they sat holding hands and saying nothing when Alice brought their soup. Frank saw the question in Alice's gaze as she brought out the sandwiches, but he didn't say anything.

"Well are you going to ask her or not?" Alice said.

"Ask me what?"

Frank pulled a tiny velvet pouch from his pocket.

"Remember I told you if I took you to lunch at Alice's that she would have us engaged before we got to the pie? It only works if you say yes." He held out a ring in his hand.

Jennita gave him her smile with the crinkles which warmed him through and through. She looked at Alice.

"I'll have the cherry pie, I think." Somehow she'd put the ring on without Frank seeing it and held it out to admire it on her hand.

"Same here, Alice," Frank said. The whole crowd cheered while Jennita leaned across the table and gave him a kiss.

***

Frank walked down Main Street. It had only been a couple of months and his shoulder was as good as new. He ducked into Alixxa's Coffee and ordered his usual black coffee.

"You really should try one of the fancy coffees," Alixxa said, "I'll even give you the first one free."

"I'm fine with this," Frank toasted her with his cup. Alice waved at him from the counter on the restaurant side of the arch. One of the new girls came through to fill the carafe and grinned at him.

"Folks are saying you should run for Mayor next year."

"Nope." Frank sipped at the hot rich coffee. "But I think your Aunt would do well."

"Come on, Aunt Alice?"

"She got the new Business Association going, convinced everyone that fixing up Main Street would be a good idea, even got old-timers and the new people talking. She'd be perfect."

"Who would run the Restaurant?"

Frank hoisted his cup at her.

"Oh no, no," Alixxa waved her hands in front of her. "I have enough on my hands with just the coffee. There's no way I want to run the whole show. You hear that Aunt Alice?" She called through the arch. "You stay out of politics and run the restaurant."

"Politics?" asked Alice.

"Frank here thinks you would make a good mayor."

"Does he now?" Alice went back to wiping the counter, but there was a thoughtful expression on her face.

"What have I done?" moaned Alixxa. She looked at Frank. "You're a terrible man. She would never have thought of it if I hadn't said anything."

"I don't know," Frank said and laughed. "But I am pretty sure someone would have mentioned it to her." He sat and finished his coffee while Alixxa served customers and peered over at her aunt.

When he finished the coffee he went back out onto the street and walked toward the library. Every store was doing business. People were bustling along the street weaving past each other in an endless dance.

"Hey Frank." John came up to him. "The plans for the development are coming along really well. Those people you put me onto are geniuses. We've already got enough people to start on the townhouses and the detached units have a waiting list. Who would have thought that giving land to parks would make you more money not less? Come by the office and I'll show you the latest plans" The younger man dashed off again before Frank could reply. The old gravel pit was in good hands.

The whistle for the shift change at the plant blew and everyone on the street paused for a second to listen. Bruce was right, the whistle reminded the folks that they owned the plant, not some far away people who didn't care about the town. They'd called back all the workers, and he'd heard that they were going to be hiring new people.

He checked his mail and said good morning to the new post mistress. He missed Jim and Mary, but Jim had got a call from a town in another state that wanted to learn how he had put together the proposal to buy the plant locally. He and Mary had moved there for the time being while he helped them work it out.

Frank arrived at the library where Greg DeLorne was sweeping the steps.

"Good morning Greg."

The young man turned his back on Frank and kept working. It was an improvement. He wasn't swearing under his breath any more. The charges against his father had been dropped, but Mrs. DeLorne had kicked her husband out and devoted her time to her new knitting shop. Greg had been given the choice of pleading out his charge and staying with his mom or fighting it and living with his dad. He chose his mom and was given probation and community service.

Frank pushed through the doors and entered the library. Sergio waved at him from the new circulation desk and pointed to the back. Frank nodded and headed back, but first he stopped at the meteorite sitting on a block in the center of the foyer. A university had mounted it in exchange for keeping the four core samples they drilled to fasten the rock down. Frank put his hand on the meteorite just as he did every day he came in. It was getting polished from other people doing the same thing.

Jennita was reading to a group of pre-schoolers in the children's room. She wiggled her eyebrows at him without missing a word in the story. Frank slid into the room and sat in a leather arm chair and listened to the sound of his wife's voice doing what she loved.

There was nowhere he would rather be.

The Heronmaster

Leaper hadn't seen the flies this thick in all the weeks since he had gotten his legs. They thickened the air and his tongue darted everywhere. He planned to eat until he was as big as Old Bull who had swallowed Jumper whole yesterday - demonstrating the importance of keeping a respectful, and safe, distance from the huge frog who ruled the pond with an iron tongue. One day it would be him sitting in that hollow stump.

"Bird!" came the call from across the pond. Leaper splashed into the warm water and peered up. A shadow passed over but didn't feel the shudder of water which meant it had landed. After a brief time, Leaper climbed back up onto the lily pad and went back to the catching of flies.

Life was good.

The afternoon passed quickly; Leaper stuffed himself with so many flies he could barely move. Under the water he soaked in warmth and oxygen in his favorite spot under a huge pad. Close enough to hear Old Bull, but far enough away to be safe from the big frog's appetite.

"Gather in," Old Bull said. "Come in close. We will sing, we will speak, we will eat." His tongue flashed out and a little frog jumped further away. Old Bull laughed and swallowed a mosquito.

The night buzzed with mosquitoes and song. Though Leaper was too young to sing the mating, he listened and wondered at the urgency of its call. It thrummed through him with a promise he felt more than understood. The old frog was talking again.

"The heron is as tall as the rushes and a lethal beak," Old Bull said, "still as death, yet deadly quick. Your only hope is to hide deep in the mud. The slightest twitch will give you away."

"Have you ever seen it?" a small frog asked.

"Come close, come close and I'll tell you how I escaped its beak."

The frog hopped a little forward and Leaper closed his eyes. He knew how this would end. Sure enough a final croak followed by Old Bull's deep chuckle came across the water.

"Be wise, young frogs. Be cautious. Eat but don't be eaten." Old Bull chuckled again, and said, "Unless it's me that's doing the eating. "

Leaper hatched from his egg knowing he'd be a meal for anything bigger than him. Anything smaller became a meal. Still, he sank under his pad and into the mud. It could have been him. It wasn't part of his plan to be a snack for another frog.

Days in the pond were all pretty much the same. Leaper lay in wait for the flies and avoided the many creatures lying in wait for him. He learned ducks weren't interested in eating frogs, but some fish were. Strange how existence could be always a matter of life and death yet also stupefyingly boring.

From the moment, he left the egg he was being chased by everything in the pond larger than him. His world was the patch of green slime on the edge of the water. Most of his egg mates vanished; eaten by fish, birds, even insects.

Leaper's first leg had been a matter of great astonishment. It didn't appear to be good for much. Flailing it about only sent him in circles. The arrival of the other leg let him swim in a straight line again. By the time he grew the front legs, his tail shrank. There was a great deal more to life than green slime. The first time he hopped out of the water and breathed air, he narrowly avoided a swoop by a kingfisher.

As the summer progressed Leaper grew in size and managed to jump a little faster or be a little luckier than his egg mates. Flies and even dragon flies formed his diet now. The days grew hotter and the water receded. What was wet muck, perfect for hiding in, became hard and cracked.

Opposite from Old Bull's stump, Leaper found a safe place. Though more than double the size he had been in the spring, the big old frog was still a danger. Leaper had seen him eat a fish yesterday.

Leaper sat with just his eyes out of the water, watching for the big juicy flies stumbling drunkenly through the late summer air. A shudder ran through the water and he froze. It didn't return, so he relaxed. Must have been the wind.

The shudder came again, smaller this time, but the sounds around him didn't change. Flies buzzed and bumbled. One of his few remaining egg mates just a couple of hops away croaked. Whatever it was seemed to be moving away.

A beautiful big fly buzzed over him and he willed it to come closer. It flew this way and that, always slightly out of reach. Leaper swam toward it. Bigger size meant bigger appetite; Leaper was always hungry. The fly would be his. He reached a shallower part of the pond and got his legs set under him. The fly came almost close enough and he jumped forward and snapped out his tongue.

His tongue struck the fly and pulled it into his mouth. His mouth closed and he swallowed the still buzzing fly. A huge beak stabbed out of the air and gripped his leg with deadly force. Leaper was lifted high into the air--caught by the heron Old Bull had talked about.

He was about to die.

Leaper tried to squirm and jump, but the bird had him tight by his leg. The fire running through his leg competed with the cold certainty of his death. The heron's predatory look measured him for a meal. Leaper thrashed about harder, but the immense bird ignored his efforts. It had no more pity for him than he had on the flies he ate. The heron tossed him into the air and Leaper saw the vicious beak stab toward him again. The frog tried to swim in the air.

The beak missed. Maybe it was the wind, or Leaper's attempts to swim in the air actually moved him. Perhaps it was luck. He bounced off the beak and dropped past the heron's eye, for a moment Leaper lay on the great bird's back. As it swung its head around to find him, Leaper rolled off and splashed into the water. The water was shallow, but the mud was soft and he buried himself deep. The shudder of the bird's feet landing shook the mud right beside him.

Leaper lay still. His leg throbbed, but he concentrated on not moving, not the slightest twitch. Would the fly's faint buzzing in his stomach betray him? After an eternity, the foot lifted and was placed down further away. Leaper lay in the mud long after the slashing movement of beak through the water told him his egg mate had been devoured. There were so few of them left.

Life was cruel.

Leaper didn't move even when the heron's feet pulled out of the mud.

After the heron left, Leaper stayed in the mud. The leg tormented him unless he held absolutely still. The slightest movement made the pain worse.

All day and through the night Leaper huddled where he lay. The pain ebbed and flowed. Each time he thought about moving, it would come back and he'd freeze up again. Hunger finally drove him out of the mud.

Leaper croaked in misery as he pushed himself from the mud into the warm water. Once he was in the water he floated and occasionally trapped a fly that came close enough. As the sun dropped below the trees, Leaper used his front legs to pull himself under a floating log where he spent the night, and the next day and the next.

His time became divided between fighting the pain of his twisted leg and trying to assuage his hunger. Leaper's leg had been broken and pulled out of its socket; swimming like a frog was impossible. Floating on the surface and paddling with his front legs was all he could do.

The remainder of the summer was a time of pain. Leaper ate, floated and tried to convince himself he was healing. He wasn't sure he believed it. The days got shorter and the flies fewer. His pain gradually faded, but never left him.

The cold days arrived and the frogs buried themselves in the mud. Leaper was able to dig himself down with his three remaining limbs. He half hoped he would be one of the ones who didn't wake up in the spring.

He froze solid from the outside in.

Ice covered the pond. Ducks waddled around on the ice before flying south. Fox and deer used the pond as a short cut. Snow covered the forest. The fox became scrawny with hunger--only the crows had enough to eat. Late in the winter even the crows starved. They picked and squabbled over bare, white bones.

***

The frogs, though, were safe under the snow. They were frozen, but not burnt by the cold. A few were too close to the surface and were dug out by raccoons.

Finally, a day was warmer than the day before, and another warmer still. The snow started melting forming rivulets on top of the ice until it dug through the ice and joined with the water below. Now the forest was about water instead of cold.

As the cold gave way to wet and then to warmth, the frogs began to thaw. They began to sing. Their song filled the woods. Frogs met, mated and laid eggs in the water spreading across the floor of the forest.

***

Leaper woke from his winter sleep and forced his way out of the mud. His leg no longer pained him, but it still didn't work well. He stayed under the log in the shade and ate whatever came past. He grew bigger than many of the frogs now, though still tiny compared to Old Bull who had emerged to rule the pond from his hollow stump.

Leaper was still unable to swim. He floated and moved himself around with his front legs, but his strong back legs were useless. One was twisted and deformed, and trying to use the opposite leg just sent him in uncontrollable circles. He couldn't hop well either. So all he did was sulk under his log and trap flies.

142

Spring crawled past. If life had been boring before he was crippled, now his life had frozen along with the joints in his left leg. The other frogs avoided Leaper because they were never sure if he was going to ignore them or try to eat them. He caught and ate a few of the young hatchlings. It was too much work to feel bad about it.

The pond went through the same changes as it had the year before. He watched the heron, or another one like it come and hunt in the pond for three days before it left. No mangled survivors remained to share Leaper's fate.

Since all Leaper did was eat and float in the pond he bloated to almost the size of Old Bull but without the muscle and speed of the old frog. Crawling out from under the log was almost impossible for him now. He didn't know what would have happened if he hadn't wakened one chilly early fall morning to find Old Bull floating beside him.

"I've been watching you." Old Bull said.

"What for?" Despite his size, Leaper tried to push further under the log.

"You're just the only frog I've ever seen survive the heron." Old Bull gave him a push. "That means something."

"What?" Leaper paddled back under the log.

"Don't know," Old Bull said, "whatever you want it to mean, I guess."

"Is it the same heron or different ones?"

"Does it matter?" Old Bull snapped up a fly with his tongue. "Did it matter to that fly whether it was you or I who ate it?"

Leaper shrugged and snapped up the next fly..

"Think about what I said," Old Bull said, and swam back to the shore. Leaper watched him swim and wondered what part of the odd conversation he was supposed to be thinking about.

The days got shorter and colder. Leaper puzzled at his conversation with the Old Bull. He didn't dare try to swim over to ask, and the old frog showed no sign of coming back to explain himself.

One particularly cold day snow fell from the grey sky. Leaper let himself sink to the bottom of the pond where he dug himself into the mud for another winter. Though his leg didn't pain him this year, he still didn't care whether he woke in the spring or not.

***

Leaper surfaced in the Spring and listened to the chorus of life echoing through the pond. He floated and looked over at the hollow stump. There was something odd about it. Evening set in before the cloud of flies around the stump grabbed his attention. Old Bull would never let that many flies gather. He paddled over to the stump and after great effort he pulled himself up into the stump. He found Old Bull's skeleton sitting there as if waiting for Leaper to come.

"So I guess this means you aren't going to explain yourself," Leaper said to the bones. He turned and looked out over the pond. The flies were still there, so he started eating them. The bones got pushed aside and somehow Leaper didn't bother to make the trip back across the pond to his log.

In the evenings, he told the young frogs the story of the heron, adding his own gruesome details to the tale Old Bull used. At first he ignored the ones who got too close. But as he watched over the pond, he saw the young frogs being careless and becoming meals. The next evening, he snapped up a young frog who hopped almost close enough to touch. The small frogs kept a more respectful distance from then on. His laugh at their fear came from his hope the survivors would be less trusting.

The stump forced him to move around more. The food no longer came to him as he floated in the water. He started hopping again. Slow and painful at first, he soon got the trick of centering his good leg behind him. A bird fell out of its nest and Leaper ate it. Even the older frogs looked at him differently after.

The warm days of summer were well upon them when a tremendous storm rocked the forest. The water ran faster and cooler when it had passed. That in itself wasn't bad. It just meant a different kind of fly mated and grew in the pond to be eaten by the frogs.

A day after the storm the Leviathan made its first appearance. Leaper was lazily snapping up flies and watching a frog swim across the pond. A sudden swirl in the water and the frog was gone. That frog wasn't the last one either. The huge fish ate frogs like they ate flies.

It was death to go near the water, but death to stay away too. The summer sun dried up all the water but in the pond. Leaper wasn't too hard off in the shade of the stump, but the pond smelled of more than one frog who had chosen to die of dehydration rather than consumption.

"Dig down into the mud," Leaper told the frogs in the evening. "Find ways to stay wet and alive." Each day more would risk jumping into the pond and the lethal swirl would show the Leviathan had eaten them.

The heron arrived and landed in the shallow water. Safe in his stump, Leaper watched with interest. There were now, two deadly creatures in the pond. The heron stalked through the weeds with impossible grace. The huge bird ate one frog, then a fish. How could any frog survive that beak? At the other end of the pond a huge shadow moved beneath the water. Nothing escaped those jaws.

Leviathan attacked as the heron swallowed another fish. With heavy swirl of water the open, toothy jaws of the great fish closed on the leg of the heron. The heron squawked and stabbed at the fish with its beak.

The pond echoed with the sound of the battle as the fish tried to pull the bird into the deep water. Blood dripped from the heron into the water, but the bird was just too big.

The heron wasn't content with trying to escape. It tried to lift off pulling the fish away from the water. The long, lethal beak struck at the fish, blood leaked from the Leviathan's eye. Water and mud splashed even as far at Leaper.

The heron was muddy and bedraggled. The fish's movement's slowed. Perhaps they would kill each other. but finally, the heron pulled loose and flew into the forest calling forlornly.

About a week after the battle between heron and fish, a new creature arrived at the pond. It stood even taller than the heron and was covered with strange growths. A small tree made it walk like it had three legs and the creature carried another branch and a small log.

The giant put the log down and opened it up and fussed with some stuff in the log, then flipped the lid closed. It reached down and plucked a small frog from under some leaves. The giant impaled the frog on a tiny stick and threw the still twitching victim into the water. It fastened a red and white rock to the thin vine connecting the dying frog to the branch in the creature's hands.

Leaper crouched down further in the stump and watched. Strange ideas moved in his head. This creature used things to make life easier. The third leg which now lay abandoned on the bank fascinated him.

The creature let the rock go out into the pond to float on the surface. It leaned back against a tree and let out a groan. Then it did nothing.

It did nothing for the rest of the day except pull things out of the log it carried and eat them. Why didn't it eat the flies buzzing in clouds around its head? Occasionally it threw away a dead frog and attached a live one in its place before throwing the thing back out into the pond.

The sun touched the trees when the red and white rock disappeared. The creature shouted and pushed itself onto its feet and began pulling on the branch, which now bent like a reed in a windstorm. At the other end of the line was the deadly swirl of the Leviathan. It had eaten the frog and was now fastened to the branch the creature held by the thinnest of vines.

In this battle of giants, Leaper hoped the strange creature would win and go back to wherever it came from.

Sometimes it seemed as if the fish was going to pull the creature into the pond, other times it was pulled toward shore. Once or twice the fish leaped out of the water and Leaper marveled that even the giant stood against such a creature.

Daylight was almost completely gone when the creature's branch broke just as the Leviathan was almost on the bank. The creature jumped into the water and grabbed hold of the fish. The Leviathan still fought, its tail beating the water and jaws gaping wide, but gradually the creature pulled the fish onto the shore. Its log was knocked aside and the remains of the branch trampled into the mud. On land the creature used its third leg to slam the fish's head. Finally, the fish lay still. The creature danced and howled around its corpse before pushing some things back into its log and putting a heavy vine through the fish's mouth and gills. It left the pieces of the thin branch and picked up its small tree, then the creature slung the Leviathan across its back and limped into the night.

In the morning, Leaper surveyed the damage from the titanic struggle. The water was stilled churned up and muddy. Plants were crushed and broken and the bodies of several frogs lay in the mud. A trail showed where the giant had left, half carrying, half dragging, the huge fish.

A host of strange things tangled in the brush beside the pond. Leaper crept out to investigate and found short vines which were smooth to the touch. He picked up a piece of the creature's branch and leaned on it as the creature had leaned on its tree. It did ease his bad leg.

He found a piece of the red and white floating rock. It was just the white with a bit of the red attached. He saw the shadow of a kingfisher, but as he lifted the piece of floating rock the bird turned away. Interesting, He put the piece on his head while he picked through the rest of the things left behind by the giant creature.

Leaper spent the rest of the day moving strange things from the bushes to his hollow stump. Some things looked like small fish or frogs but with cruel hooked teeth. Those were what the frogs had been impaled on. He shuddered, and placed them carefully, not wanting to stick himself on the barbed teeth. Other things were shiny vines, and plenty of the thin vine. Other things too, which the frog had no words to describe. The creature carried these things here, so they must be valuable, not purposefully left behind.

Leaper held the odd pieces and turned them over in his hands. They could be attached together, or taken apart. The vine attached to the pieces with a tangle, but always the same way. Leaper taught himself to tie and untie the tangles.

Summer waned and the extra flow to the pond meant it didn't dry up as much as before. Now, the Leviathan was gone the frogs returned to the water gratefully. There weren't many left.

"Dig deep into the mud, this cold season," he said when the frogs gathered. "Our only defense against monsters is to have more tadpoles. We must fill the pond with frogs again.

Between fish and bird and giant they had suffered a great deal. The frogs were at the mercy of whatever predators happened their way. Losing the slow and the foolish was part of life, but the Leviathan and the giant had taken even the swift. Another summer like this one and there might not even be a remnant left. Yet he survived, and sat in the Old Bull's stump. What else might life offer?

Leaper buried the strange collection of things he'd taken from where the giant had dropped them. Then he dug deep into the mud, for the first time he wanted to make it through the winter.

***

The snows came, and the frost. The winter passed as it always did. Most survived and some did not. Leaper was one of the first to climb out of the mud and join the song more alive than he'd been since the day of the heron.

The song made this spring different. The croaking music pulled at him and set his blood on fire. Leaper had sulked under the log after his first winter, and wakened late his second. Now he was awake and fiercely focused on the need to repopulate the pond.

Leaper sent his bass voice out over the pond and waited for females to respond. Other species croaked and squeaked and called too. He'd never experienced anything like it. The call filled him and made him forget his twisted leg as he put his whole being into his song.

A female hopped up tentatively and another male bullfrog, Hopper, came out of the reeds to mount her. Leaper roared and threw himself at his rival. They banged up against each other. The other frog was smaller, but Leaper's bad leg made it an even match. After one crashing blow, Leaper's hand fell on a short length of reed. He picked it up and used it to balance himself. This time he overpowered his smaller rival. The other frog fled while Leaper mounted the female.

Leaper won battle after battle for the females vaguely aware other bullfrogs were mating in other places around the pond, but he ruled the stump and the space around it. There would be lots of eggs this year. Lots of tadpoles, and many more frogs the year after.

The end of the song and the mating season left Leaper exhausted and content. He didn't have long to rest. The extra flow of water brought more fish to the pond. Small fish - fish that liked frog's eggs. Leaper jumped into the water and tried to catch the fish, but with his leg he was too slow. Instead he positioned himself near the eggs and snapped up fish like flies.

"We must protect the eggs," Leaper said from his stump. The fish are as good as flies.

"You will just eat us," one of the smaller frogs called from the pond.

"There are lots of eggs and even more fish. I will not eat frogs when I can eat fish. We need the eggs to survive.

For a week, they gorged on fish. Suddenly, they stopped coming and at the same time the extra flow of water ceased. It was a good sign. The fish were tasty, but too much trouble. Time the pond went back to normal.

The eggs hatched and the tadpoles fended for themselves. Some would start growing legs within weeks, but the bullfrog tadpoles would take two years. Last year's hatchlings were huge in comparison and voracious in appetite. Leaper left them. It was up to them now to make the shift from tadpole to frog.

Maybe it was all the fish Leaper and the other frogs ate when they were protecting the eggs, but he'd never seen so many little frogs trying to make sense of the world beyond the water. He even restrained himself and ate only the truly slow and foolish ones. In a matter of weeks, the pond went from being bare to crawling with a myriad of tiny frogs. They were hungry too. Leaper hardly ate a fly without almost tangling tongues with some minute hopper. They were cute; he just wished they weren't such a nuisance.

A pair of kingfishers had built a nest high above the pond. They swooped down, snatching up frogs and minnows with equal ease. The kingfisher eggs had hatched and the nestlings were being fed constantly by their attentive parents. Leaper watched, but they were barely making a dent in the horde of frogs crawling out of the pond.

Spring was giving way to summer and there was a pleasant buzz of flies around. The day the nestlings learned to fly. a tiny bird slashed across the air and looped back to its nest. Another followed, then another, until the air was full of tiny swooping birds. The spectacle was repeated the next day and the next. By the end of the week the little birds learned how to hunt. At first it was funny, they would splash into the water and come out with a minnow or tadpole in their beaks, often nothing.

The first one to snatch a frog from the shore dropped its prey before it got back to the branch. It returned, but instead of retrieving the dying frog from the ground it took a different one, and dropped it too. Soon all the tiny birds were attacking frogs and dropping mortally wounded prey all over the pond.

The kingfishers had ducked away from the white and red thing from the giant's log. He dug it up and found a length of the thin branch with a sharp point on one end and a loop to hold on to to ease his leg. Leaper jumped into the middle of the fray, but the small birds paid no attention to the covering. The parent birds called to their young, but the swarm didn't stop. One dove to attack Leaper and he lifted his branch to ward it off. The young kingfisher impaled itself on the point. Its shrieks cut through the air and reached the young birds in a way the adult scolding had not. The rest of the flock attacked Leaper.

He pulled his branch from the still flapping kingfisher and waved it at the other birds. They twisted out of the way and darted back in trying to stab him with their beaks. He knocked one out of the air and it rolled on the ground shrieking like its now still nest mate. The rest continued their attack. Leaper crouched down and braced himself for a moment. Then he launched himself straight up and snatched a bird out of the air like it was a fly. The rest of the young kingfishers vanished into the tree. Leaper swallowed the bird, then he ate the dead one. The last still fluttered on the ground, trying to escape him with a broken wing.

Leaper looked up into the tree to catch the eyes of the remaining birds before he gulped down the still living bird. The day of the heron a fly buzzed in his stomach, today a bird--for the first time since he found the bones of Old Bull in the stump he felt like he ruled the pond.

Back at his stump he left the red and white thing on his head and leaned the branch close at hand. Old Bull told stories; Leaper would hunt to protect his pond. Crippled or not it was his responsibility.

The kingfishers hunted the fish in the pond, but never again attacked the frogs on the shore. Their small birds grew bigger and eventually vanished from the pond. The frogs ate flies and minnows and anything else that was foolish enough to get too close to them. Flies weren't enough for Leaper anymore, so he hunted mice and other tiny creatures in the woods around the pond. With his white and red head covering and the branch, the other frogs gave him a respect, and a distance, greater than he'd given Old Bull.

***

Then the herons arrived and everything changed again.

Leaper expected the single heron that came each year. But this year the trees filled with herons. They stalked through the water eating fish and frog with impunity. The herons wouldn't be scared by Leaper's head covering. Yet again, the frogs cowered under whatever safety they found. The only freedom was found at night when the herons slept.

Leaper was hunting through the woods when he spotted a spider web glinting in the moonlight. He'd seen plenty of spider webs, and eaten his share of spiders. What caught his attention this night was the huge moth struggling in the web. As he munched on the moth, he wished he there was a web large enough to trap a heron. The rest of the bits and pieces from the creature's log, perhaps he could make one.

Leaper sat in his stump and held the pieces in his hands, especially taken by the smooth ones with rings at each end. There should be a way to form them into a web. The herons stalked through his pond as he worked with the oddments. He needed one thing to hold its deadly beak shut. Another to control the head. A way of managing a creature many times bigger than he was. He wasn't sure what he was going to do if he did capture a heron. Even he couldn't eat it. Though given half a chance he was willing to try.

Leaper fashioned a web he thought would work. Now he had to figure out how to make it happen. The heron wasn't going to just stand and wait for him to catch it with his tangle of oddities. The spider wove its web and waited for the fly to get stuck. Only when the insect was well and truly caught did the spider come to claim its prey. Leaper's web wasn't big enough to hold a heron, nor was it sticky like the spider web. He tried throwing it, but it tangled, As he picked up his web from one of his attempts a sharp pain stabbed his foot. When he jerked his foot back, he pulled a strange copy of a frog from under the leaves--one of the creature's things. He thought of the battle with the huge fish and had the beginning of a plan.

Leaper laid out his web carefully on the surface of the lily pads before the sun rose. He watched from his stump. The birds avoided the web. If he had enough he could make the pond safe just by spreading over the whole of the water. But the idea was to trap a heron, not scare it away. He banged the soft floor of his stump in frustration.

For this to work the web had to be as invisible as a spider web.

The next night he tried fastening it to the underside of the lily pads using bits of the creature's thin vine. Once again the birds stayed away from where the net lurked. He moved the net again and tried it in the midst of tall weeds. Again, the herons avoided it. Leaper gave up in disgust. He was, after all a frog, not a spider. Maybe if he wielded a tree instead of a piece of a branch he would be able to stab a heron as he had the young kingfishers. He let the net lie and went back to planning.

He sulked through the next day as the herons ate their fill from his pond. One of them walked very close to the web before veering off. Old Bull had sat very still for a long time before he lunged to the attack. Patience and surprise were key. By the third day of the web lying in the weeds the herons ignored it. That night he moved it to where he wanted it. It only took a couple of days before the herons were once again stalking past the web with no fear. The web did nothing and they were too busy consuming frogs and fish to be deterred for long by something as limp and harmless as this web.

At night, Leaper set the rest of his trap. Before the sun rose over the trees, he took his place under the log where he'd hidden after his first encounter with a heron. Leaper couldn't remember being that isolated and uncaring frog. From here his web and most of the pond were visible. What was more, the vibrations in the mud and the water told him where the heron hunted. In his hand, he held the vine; like spider web it was so thin and hard to see. Now for patience.

From Leaper's observations, the herons all followed one particular bird. bigger than the rest. That bird must be to the herons as Leaper was to the frogs. Control the big one and, he hoped, control the flock.

Lesser herons stalked past and Leaper didn't move. He waited all day, but the big heron didn't come near. The next day was the same. The herons had staked out territories and the biggest heron was on the other side of the pond where it would be much more difficult to lay the trap.

When night fell, Leaper took the branch he used to hunt birds and mice, then swam to the other side and scouted out the new territory. Even as the head of the pond he didn't come here much; swimming with his one good leg was slow and cumbersome. He set out his web and took up position below a large lily pad. This was much more risky. If the bird saw him, it would snap him up as easily as it would eat a tadpole.

"What are you doing here?" Hopper floated over to Leaper. "Aren't you content with ruling the pond, must you hunt my territory too?"

"How much hunting have you done since the herons arrived?" Leaper paddled until he looked the other frog in the eye.

"Not enough." Hopper's eye took on a predatory gleam. "You aren't as scary in the water."

Leaper swung his branch until it just touched Hopper below the eye.

"I don't want to eat you, it would slow me down. I'm after bigger prey."

"I was wrong." Hopper back paddled quickly. "You're terrifying." He pointed to the trees. "Do you really think you can hunt a heron?"

"If I'm wrong, you will live in the stump and rule the pond."

Hopper started to swim away.

"You are still too small, Hopper," Leaper called to him. "Hunt the woods, eat bigger prey, become terrifying in your own way. If you want the stump, you must be ready."

Hubris and hope kept Leaper company until the sun rose.

The sun stood high in the sky before the herons dropped out of the trees to hunt the pond. There was less for them to eat. The abundance of frogs in the spring had been brutally thinned by the herons.

That thinning would end today.

The herons, especially the biggest, were masters of patience. They stood completely still until frog or fish made a move. Then the heron struck like lightning before tossing the prey only to swallow and wait for its next victim. To cause the least amount of vibration in the water, the heron moved one foot at a time very slowly.

Leaper decided they were strongest when they were slow. They had time to think and plan. It was during their flashing attack they were vulnerable, but only if he avoided the beak. Under his lily pad, line in hand, Leaper waited, ready to pounce. Frogs too, knew how to move with deadly swiftness.

He had snatched a bird out of the air. He was a predator.

The heron landed in the water near Leaper and stood still until the ripples of its landing passed. It lifted a leg and slowly placed it back in the water nearer Leaper, then stood still again. Another step, another pause.

The heron towered over Leaper now. He wondered how it didn't know to stab its beak through the lily and capture him. I could leave and go back to my stump. Then the beak did come down, but not into the lily, it snatched up a small fish and swallowed. The heron took a step and blocked out the light of the sun. Leaper felt rather than saw when the heron's head was in the right place. I won't deserve the stump if I don't do this. He pulled on the line in his hand and the sharp toothed frog like thing from the creature's log followed the line into the sunlight.

The heron's beak stabbed down into the water, through the center of the web Leaper had spread the night before. He was already pulling the web tight around the beak as the huge bird threw its head up to swallow. The line yanked Leaper out of the water and he was just able to hold on. The not-frog with the barbed teeth caught in the heron's beak near where the web trapped it shut. Leaper held on to the web until, for the second time in his life, he landed on the back of a heron. This time he didn't roll off.

He pulled at the web and forced the heron's head toward its neck. Leaper jumped away and the line pulled him back, but he'd swung around the heron's neck. The bird tried to swing its beak free. Leaper used the motion to wrap more line around the heron's neck and beak. The heron began to flap its wings and stagger in the water, but it couldn't escape. The web was tight, the trap closed. Leaper took hold of the branch on his next swing. He climbed the the web until he was in the heron's line of sight, then pointed his branch with its bloody point at the heron's throat.

"Yield or die," he said, and suddenly felt foolish since he was sure the heron wouldn't understand him. Yet the heron dropped its head and stood still.

He'd done it! He'd trapped the heron. Leaper still from the tangle of the web and line tangled around the heron.

Now what I do?

He crawled back onto the heron's back and studied the mess. He started to untangle the lines so the heron could move again. It was hard to do one handed so he slung his branch over his back and went to work. He was half finished when his bad leg slipped and sent him tumbling off the heron's back. He landed on a lily pad and lay stunned. The big heron called out and Leaper watched another heron appear beside him and lean down.

This is it, I'm done now. The branch was no help, since he'd landed on it and felt it snap beneath him; at least he hoped it was the branch. It wouldn't matter in a second anyway.

The second heron didn't eat him, but put its beak beside him in what had to be an uncomfortable position with the beak flat on the pad beside him. It waited.

164

Leaper pulled himself together and climbed onto the beak. He was lifted gently back to the trapped heron's back where he finished his untangling job. He stood unsteadily on the heron's back and looked out over the pond. All the herons faced him; as one, they dropped their heads in submission.

Leaper was going to just drop the tangle into the water but slung the mess over his shoulder instead, and pointed toward his hollow stump. The heron walked around the pond, then knelt until Leaper slid off onto the ground. He turned and looked the heron in the eye and pantomimed eating, then pointed at himself, then around the pond. He made a sharp motion with his hand. The heron bowed until its beak touched the ground in front of Leaper, then it stood up and made a loud call; the other herons flew up into the trees.

The big heron stood right there like it planned to stand there all night. Leaper shrugged the web off his shoulder and dragged it into his stump to untangled it.

How do I keep from falling off the heron? He needed something to hang on to. Part of the web would go on the beak and head. If he changed things just a little the heron would be able to use its beak to feed. Didn't want the bird getting too hungry. Would be nice to be as comfortable on the heron as in his stump. His bad leg made standing painful, maybe some kind of platform to sit on?

Leaper climbed out of the stump and hopped toward where the creature had dropped all the strange stuff. Maybe he had missed something. He needed a new branch anyway.

A new piece of the giant's branch poked out from the weeds. When Leaper tugged at it, The loop caught in overhead branches and when Leaper freed it there were more things caught in the bushes above him. They'd been there almost a year and still hadn't rotted. Leaper took whatever he could. He turned around to see a raccoon eying him. It licked its chops and began walking forward as if Leaper were dead. With all the stuff dangled about him, he might as well have been.

The frog was furious at himself. How could he be this careless?

If he was going to go, he wasn't going to go without a fight. Leaper dropped everything he was carrying and let out a roar. He charged at the raccoon like it was another bullfrog after his mate. The animal's eyes widened for a moment, then its mouth dropped open as if it expected Leaper to crawl right in. Instead Leaper clamped his mouth hard on the animal's nose. An instant later. the heron's massive foot came down on the raccoon's tail. It shook its head and flung Leaper into the bushes, then yanked its tail away from the heron and ran into the woods whimpering as it went.

The heron's eye peered at Leaper as he dragged himself from the bush. The heron nodded once, then started to move the pile of things Leaper had collected to the stump. Leaper picked up his branch and limped back to the stump. He climbed in and went to sleep. Leaper had no idea why the heron had made itself his protector, but he wasn't going to complain.

Sometime in the night, while his pond mates were cavorting in the water and singing in celebration, the jumble of things from the creature's horde came together in Leaper's mind. When he woke, he climbed out of the stump and began seeing if his vision would work. There was a soft flat thing with loops on both ends. If that would go over the heron's back with something to hold it on, he'd steady himself with his feet. The trap could be fixed with some extra lines to give direction to the heron.

It took a couple of days for Leaper to arrange everything to his satisfaction. During those two days, the herons stayed in the trees except for the one who watched over Leaper. The leader let them down one at a time to feed on fish in the pond. Not one touched a frog

Ignoring how foolish he would look if this didn't work, Leaper waved at the heron which towered over him and signaled for it to kneel. The immense bird immediately crouched down. Leaper tried to lift the flat piece up high enough, but even crouched to the ground the heron's back was too high. It was watching Leaper though, and gave a brief hoot. Another heron flew over and landed beside them. After a brief exchange, it lifted the stuff onto the bigger heron's back. Leaper crawled around and fastened things until he was sure it wasn't all going to slide off the moment he climbed up.

He fetched his white and red covering for his head and his branch, then clambered up onto the seat on the heron's back. He took hold of the lines that went to the web around the bird's beak and head and gave a little tug. The heron turned to look at him and Leaper pointed up. The heron stood and Leaper surveyed the pond from a whole new angle. He'd been too concerned with not falling off to pay much attention before.

At one end, a ridge of mud and sticks held back water. Below that, water wound into the distance with weeds and trees on either side. Frogs often wandered up and down the bank, especially at mating time. In the other direction, there were again weeds and brush along winding water. In the distance were the faint outline of another ridge of mud and branch. The world was a much bigger place than his pond. Time to see more of it.

The heron walked around the pond, slowly at first, then quicker as it became clear that Leaper wasn't going to fall off.

The heron gave a call and the other herons flew out of the trees to land around them. Then they started to walk downstream from the pond.

"Wait!" Leaper said. He tugged on one line and the heron turned to look at him. Leaper pointed to a place in the pond. Not far from where he had trapped the heron. The bird walked over, then looked at Leaper who motioned the bird to crouch. Hopper sat in the mud with just his head out of the water.

"You're in charge," Leaper pointed at the stump. The other frog's mouth dropped open and Hopper stared at Leaper. A fly came out of his mouth and Leaper laughed. He signaled up to the heron and they walked away from the pond.

Leaper didn't look back.
***

They followed the water. One of the herons made a quick snatch and then suddenly looked around with a frog caught in its beak. All the rest stopped and stared at it, then looked back at Leaper.

"I can't let you starve," Leaper said, though he was sure they didn't understand him. "Eat the slow and the foolish. It is the way it is." He accompanied his speech with what he thought was the opposite of the sharp negation he had used earlier. The heron he rode must have understood his intent because it gave a short call. The heron with the frog bowed deeply, then swallowed the frog. From then on as they walked, the herons hunted fish or frog.

They walked all day, then instead of resting in the trees, they formed a circle around Leaper, who took a much needed swim, then fell asleep instantly. He woke once in the night to see the herons gathered around him then went back to sleep without thinking how strange it was he took comfort from their presence.

The next day he made them stop more often for him to swim; more prey at ground level too. The herons hunted while he rested, but always one stood over him. At the end of that day they reached a body of water which made his pond look tiny indeed. The water stretched as far as he could see even from the back of the heron.

Each heron took flight as it reached the big water. They circled above until Leaper's heron reached the shore. It looked back at Leaper. He swallowed and pointed up. Without any other warning the heron leaped into the air and the entire flock headed across the water.

Once they were in the air, the edges of immense pond expanded in every direction. The herons headed to a bit of land sitting in the water like an giant lily pad. When they reached it the other herons circled around until Leaper's heron had landed on the shore. As soon as they touched down the others flew away back the way they had come.

The heron took Leaper along the shore. It acted more like prey than a hunter now. The slowness of its steps weren't to look down for food, but around at the rocks and logs on the shore. Leaper didn't want to meet what would eat the heron. They followed the shoreline with the waves washing over the heron's feet. A huge rock up ahead, lay half in and half out of the water.

Then the rock moved.

There were small turtles in the pond, hardly big enough to eat tadpoles. This giant turtle would snap up Leaper and hardly notice, could eat the heron and still be hungry. Still, the heron walked closer. It stopped a few good hops away from the turtle and crouched down. Leaper slid off the heron and let himself slump to the ground. He waited until his leg started feeling normal again, then waited a little longer. The turtle had shifted so its back was to Leaper and the heron. Leaper pried himself up with his branch and hopped a little closer to the turtle. The heron stirred nervously but didn't move any closer.

A fire flamed to life in Leaper. Not the desperation which led him to capture the heron, nor the fury which made him attack the raccoon, this was a need to be seen. He'd accomplished the impossible, the turtle would acknowledge him, even if it meant his end.

Another hop closer and Leaper gave a roar. The turtle spun faster than Leaper had imagined possible and a head snapped forward. Leaper leaned on his branch and waited for death. Instead the turtle stopped close enough for Leaper to touch its face. A strange sound came from the turtle.

"You've brought me a strange one, Spearbeak," the turtle rumbled, and Leaper realized it was laughing.

"My name is Leaper."

"I can see that," the turtle said, "and your mind leaps higher than your legs. I am Grandmother Turtle. Spearbeak has brought you here for me to teach you to speak."

"We are speaking," Leaper said.

"But you're talking to me," the turtle said, "and all creatures can talk to me. You need to be able to talk to Spearbeak and she to you."

172

"Why couldn't we before?"

"Would you converse with the flies you eat?" Grandmother Turtle sounded sad.

"What would they say to me?" Leaper asked.

The turtle laughed again and shook her head. "Not much you would care to hear. Come, follow me."

Leaper hopped along after Grandmother Turtle; the heron, Spearbeak, followed too. They reached a rock wall rising up further than Leaper's sight. The turtle stretched up and scratched the rock. Dust fell on her, but she kept scratching. Gradually her scratches took shape; a frog with an odd shaped head. It was him, he touched the head covering. The turtle kept scratching and now it was Spearbeak, with the web and the other stuff Leaper had fastened to her.

The Grandmother Turtle breathed on the drawings.

"Now you can talk to each other, for as long as you live. So, you may have all the words you need, I've given you the human's language. You may not find it a blessing." She walked away and left the two alone.

Leaper turned and looked at the heron.

"I am Leaper." He leaned on his branch, spear his mind corrected him.

"Spearbeak" the heron stretched tall and spread his wings.

"Why did you herons come in such numbers to my pond?"

"It was safe," Spearbeak said.

"A fish almost ate one of your flock last summer."

"Scratchlegs," Spearbeak said. "He told us of his battle."

"He won," Leaper said.

"He escaped," Spearbeak said, shaking her head. "If he'd won, he'd have eaten fish for a lifetime."

"We called it Leviathan," Leaper sat on a rock. "A giant creature came and caught it after a long fight and dragged it off into the woods."

"A human." The heron fell silent for a long time. "I wondered when I saw the hat you wore."

Leaper put his hand to his head.

"Your spear too," she said. "As sharp and swift as my beak. I knew, when I saw your spear at my throat, you were our only hope. We need your help."

"You'd better explain." Leaper rubbed his twisted leg.

The heron crouched. "We can talk as easily while I carry you."

Leaper climbed up on the heron. How quickly the strange became comfortable. The heron took off and headed back across the lake.

"The humans," Spearbeak said, "are poisoning us. We went to our nesting grounds which have been ours since the beginning, but started to get sick. Our young died first, then the old. I finally had to take my flock and leave. Scratchlegs led us to your pond. We were hungry from fear of eating at the nesting grounds."

"The slow and the foolish," Leaper said, "are rightful prey, but so many herons were going to eat every last frog in the pond."

"The humans' poison made us act like them."

Sparkling water passed beneath them. Dark trees lined the shore. Hard to imagine poison to threaten the herons in such a view. The flock waited where the creek met the lake. Spearbeak landed in front of a heron.

"Scratchlegs, lead the flock further from the humans until I return. I take the Heronmaster to see the poison."

The other heron nodded. Now he knew the story, the lack of young and old was clear. The fear which lay on them was familiar. He'd known it sitting in his stump while fish and heron consumed his kind.

Spearbeak took off again and flew away with Leaper across the lake. Words for things he'd never seen before floated into his head. Amusing until he saw the boat and the humans.

"We should be safe up here," Spearbeak said, "Even most humans leave us alone." She flew on for a while then pointed out a strange thing on the shore. It looked like an ant colony gone mad, village his mind supplied. In the centre was a circle of green like a lily pad in the midst of grey rock, park.

"The humans live there," Spearbeak circled above the town, as people pointed up at them. "They dirty their own nests, but that is nothing compared to what they do to our nesting ground."

"Show me," Leaper said.

"That's next." Spearbeak headed away from the village "but we will stop to rest and eat before we go. You mustn't eat so much as a fly while you are there."

She stopped at a tiny marsh beside the lake and stalked fish while Leaper ate flies and whatever else he caught.

"I didn't see any frogs," he said.

"The humans hunt them," Spearbeak said.

Leaper shuddered, the humans would be much worse than even a flock of herons.

The sun sank behind the trees, so Spearbeak took Leaper to a tiny pond deep in the woods. A beer can glinted from the bottom of the pond. No frogs sang and few animals moved in the woods. Leaper slept poorly. He dreamed for the first time.

He grew huge in size and burst out of his frog skin to become a human who put a tiny Spearbeak on a hook to catch a giant fish.

"All these words in my head are worse than swallowing a live bee," Leaper said, "I'm never sure if one will sting me."

"I think I understand," Spearbeak crouched for Leaper to climb into his saddle.

They flew further away from the town until Leaper they reached a forest of dead trees.

"There is our nesting ground," Spearbeak said with a mix of pride and sorrow in her voice. She circled low, the bones of herons shone white against the dark mud.

"Is there anything of the humans here?"

"One thing." Spearbeak headed upstream to where the river widened and the bottom was gravel. A barrel sat on one bank. Black liquid leaked out of the bottom. Spearbeak landed in a tree on the river bank.

"This is as close as I dare come." Leaper didn't answer. He was thinking of the human carrying a tackle box by the handle. Even a human wouldn't be able to easily carry this barrel. But there were eight loops on the rim something could catch those loops and lift it up.

"We'll need ropes and hooks," Leaper said, "and lots of help."

"The humans will have rope," Spearbeak said, "but it will be dangerous."

"You're right," Leaper said, "but it will be the easy part."

They flew back to the flock, and Spearbeak explained to the rest of the herons what Leaper needed.

Before the sun rose they took to the air and flew to the town. The herons picked up every loose bit of rope they found, before flying away toward the nesting grounds. A few humans ran out of their houses to point and shout at the retreating birds.

Spearbeak had them stop well short of the poisoned ground.

Leaper sorted the ropes, picking and choosing until he had eight ropes which would do. Eight herons picked up the ropes while Spearbeak carried Leaper, and they headed upriver to where the human's poison was seeping into the river.

"Have them drop the ropes on the barrel, then wait in the trees," Leaper said, "You'll have to drop me on the barrel, then go wait with them."

"I will help you," Spearbeak said.

"Can you tie knots?" Leaper asked. "There will be danger enough by the end. There is no need for you to risk death too."

"I will help you."

"Very well, but stay clear of the poison."

The herons tried, but the ropes wouldn't stay on the barrel. Spearbeak had to hold them while Leaper peered at the knots which attached the leaders to form the heron's harness. He had to tie eight knots and he needed to get them right. The fumes on the barrel made his skin burn, but he tied and checked each knot.

They would only get one chance at this.

Finally, the knots were done, but Leaper was in agony and almost blind from the poison.

"Call the herons, don't let them any closer than they need to be to grasp the ropes." Leaper's voice was a rasping croak. Spearbeak called to the other herons. He barely felt the heron's beak gently pick him up and put him in his saddle.

"We fly to the town. We can't stop or we might poison the whole lake."

"Then what?" Spearbeak asked as they lifted off.

"We give them back their poison. Even the humans must have someone wise enough to know what to do with it."

The herons gripped the ropes and struggled to take off. Leaper feared they would injure themselves, but the herons finally lifted the barrel away from where it sat and head up into the sky and toward the human's town.

As they flew the moving air eased the burning in Leaper's skin. Only shadows of the herons flying as Spearbeak encouraged her flock told Leaper they were there. The sun shone down on Leaper's back. Back at his pond he would be soaking in the warmth and eating flies. Maybe he'd talk to the new frogs, telling them tales of huge fish and herons and humans.

Poison ran in his veins now, absorbed through his skin from the black liquid in the barrel. He used all his strength to hold on to Spearbeak.

"We are at the human town," Spearbeak said, "Where should we put it?"

"Find the park, a patch of green like a lily pad," Leaper said, "It is the heart of their town. We leave it there."

He felt the herons slow and circle down until the barrel touched the ground. Then the herons carrying the ropes flew away. The people shouted behind them.

"Were those great blue herons carrying that drum?" a man said.

"Careful, it's marked poison!" a woman said

"Is a frog riding that heron?" the man spoke again.

"Maybe it's a Heronmaster!" a child called out.

"Call the police, they'll know what to do with the poison," the woman said

"I'm thinking someone needs to check out the heron nesting grounds. It's near the old quarry, if someone's dumping there it would poison the whole lake," a different man said.

"See," Leaper whispered, "Someone wise enough."

Spearbeak flew up and away from the town.

"I'll get you to some clean water and you'll be fine," Spearbeak said.

"Take my hat and my spear back to my pond," Leaper said.

The heron went still and glided through the summer sky. The sun's warmth didn't reach the chill settling into him. Freezing solid for the winter didn't bother him, yet here in the sun, he shivered.

"It will be done," she said.

They circled down and landed. The other herons called to them. Spearbeak called back. He didn't have the will to sort out what they said.

"There is lots of marsh around the pond," Leaper said. "You can take your flock there until the poison is gone from your nesting grounds."

"I will tell Scratchlegs," Spearbeak said, "You are my Heronmaster, and I will stay with you."

"What is a Heronmaster?" Leaper asked.

"You are," Spearbeak said, "we named you, the human child named you."

"Take me where I will not poison what comes after me." His hat and spear were gently taken from him by heron beaks.

"Scratchlegs will lead you to a new nesting ground," Spearbeak said to her flock. "Then spread across the land to hunt. It is not wise to eat all the prey in one place."

He barely noticed her take off.

They flew for a while until Spearbeak glided into a gentle landing. She walked along the beach until Leaper saw Grandmother Turtle. He couldn't see anything else; as if she was more real than the rest of the world.

"Back so soon?" she asked.

"I've done what I needed to do, Grandmother," Leaper said. "I've come to die where the poison in me will do no more harm."

"The poison is in both of us," Spearbeak said. The heron had stood patiently next to him, handing him ropes, breathing in the toxic fumes around the barrel.

"We came to end our lives with you and each other."

"My children," Grandmother said, "who said this was the end?"

And she laughed.

***

Hopper sat in the stump worrying Leaper was going to come back and kick him out. The herons dropped out of the sky around him and he shrank back into the stump. Leaper put me here. Hopper jumped out at them.

All the herons bent their heads to him. Then one put Leaper's strange white and red head covering beside him, another placed Leaper's branch down. Hopper looked at the things then up at the herons.

The herons nodded at him once more, then flew away, spreading out as they went until they vanished behind the trees.

Hopper jumped back up into the hollow stump. He caught a fly that came too close, and surveyed his pond.

Life was good.

The Illustrator

Wil Oberdier is a freelance illustrator and fine artist who makes his home in Shelby, Ohio. Experiment is the advice he gives to up and coming students of art and illustration. Wil's unmistakable combination of painting and textures over a loose pencil sketch gives his work mystery and depth beyond the surface of the canvas.

He is a frequent contributor on Worth1000.com where he serves as an administrator for the illustration arena. He has won numerous awards of merit both at home and online. More of Wil's work can be seen at wilustration.com.

Acknowledgements

The Heronmaster wouldn't exist if it weren't for Wil's art and a contest on Worth1000.com. I'm honoured to be using the picture which inspired the story as a cover for this collection.

The stories here are a wide range of ages, but all have been through the crucible of Worth1000.com. While I'm not as active there as I once was, I still remember it as a place where I started making the shift from a hobby writer to selling my books.

Two other websites have had an impact on the work you read. Wattpad.com has given me the chance to put out draft copies and get valuable feedback. Critique Circle, my newest favourite site has done the same with a more intense focus.

Of course, it wouldn't be possible to write so much as a page without the ongoing support of my wife and muse, Alexandra Béasse.

Alex's other Books

Wendigo Whispers

The Devil Reversed

Generation Gap

The Gods Above

Tales of Light and Dark

Like Mushrooms (poetry and photography)

The Heronmaster

Blood and Sparkles, and other stories

Princess of Boring

By the Book

Sarcasm is My Superpower

Playing on Yggdrasil

The Unenchanted Princess

Alex also has stories in:

Words on the Rocks

Beyond the Wail

Collidor Stream Collection 2016